Charlie's Christmas Carole

by

Diana Stout

DEDICATION

To those who still believe in the magick.

CONTENTS

INTRODUCTION

I grew up fascinated by books. I'd read by a pen flashlight and every time it was taken away, I'd read by the streetlight that streamed through the window until I could buy my next penlight. I'd read while walking home from school, between classes, in the car, and other spare moments.

And then, I fell in love with movies. My first favorite was and is the 1944, *The Uninvited* with Ray Milland. I became a movie junkie—from the classics of yesteryear to today's modern blockbuster sure to become classics for another generation. Even today, movies starring Gregory Peck, Susan Hayward, Rock Hudson, Doris Day, Charlton Heston, Cary Grant, Clark Gable, and Maureen O'Hara are still my favorites.

Today, writing screenplays is my favorite medium to create.

My dream is that somewhere along this fabulous writing journey that one of my published scripts will end up in the hands of someone who can bring the story to the screen, big or small—a life-long dream for this writer.

Enjoy!

Diana Stout
December 13, 2022

Charlie's Christmas Carole

Fade In:

EXT. MISTLETOE, GEORGIA — DAY – WINTER

Small town. Christmas decorations being removed from downtown. A few PEDESTRIANS, light traffic. Moss draped, huge, live oaks and pines. Balmy, only a lightweight jacket needed.

Several houses, located side by side, mass of trees behind yards becomes a dense forest.

EXT. BACKYARD — DAY

YOUNG CAROLE CULLEN and YOUNG CHARLIE DICKENS, both nine years old, walk toward the woods, pulling a sled with wheels.

Suddenly, Carole puts a hand on Charlie's arm, stops him. She points ahead. Pure fascination.

> YOUNG CAROLE
>
> Look!

He does. Sees reindeer with enormous antlers and a bent ear. It stomps, nods his head.

> YOUNG CHARLIE
>
> His ear is bent.

> YOUNG CAROLE
>
> Bently. His name is Bently.

Bently nods again. Steps forward and looks up.

Immediately, large flakes of snow begin to fall.

Carole and Charlie look up.

Charlie holds out his hand, trying to catch one.

Carole sticks out her tongue and giggles as one lands on the tip of her tongue.

They grab each other's hands and twirl around in a circle, laughing.

They stop and Carole looks around.

                    CAROLE
          Bently! He's gone!

Charlie looks around too. Not seeing Bently, he looks at Carole, his eyes wide.

                    CHARLIE
          Where'd it go?

                    CAROLE
          It was magic.

                    CHARLIE
          Yeah.

EXT. SIDEYARD BETWEEN HOUSES – FEW DAYS LATER

Young Charlie and Young Carole stand between their two houses, face each other with sad faces.

From the forest, Bently comes into the clearing. His attention on the two children.

b.g. Out on street, MAN shuts moving van doors.

Loaded car behind van. MOTHER, standing by car, watches doors being shut.

                    YOUNG CAROLE
          Will I ever see you again?

                    YOUNG CHARLIE
          No.

Young Carole notices Bently.

                    YOUNG CAROLE
          Bently came to say goodbye.

Young Charlie doesn't look.

Bently snorts, stomps the ground.

Young Charlie refuses to look.

CHARLIE'S MOTHER

Come on, Charlie. It's time to go.

Charlie turns and walks toward car. Mother gets behind the wheel.

Charlie gets in backseat and stares out back window at Carole. Car moves away.

INT. CAR

CHARLIE'S POV - Carole, small and alone stands in middle of yard. She waves.

EXT. YARD

CAROLE'S POV - Charlie, looking out back window, waves back.

CAROLE

(to herself)
I won't forget you, Charlie.

She turns, wipes a tear, walks to Bently.

CAROLE

He saw you but refuses to believe anymore.
Something happened.

Bently shakes its head. Nuzzles Carole.

CUT TO:

EXT. PENNSYLVANIA — HALLOWEEN — PRESENT DAY – 25 YEARS LATER

Leaves in peak color, vibrant and rich.

EXT. ANY TOWN PENNSYLVANIA — NEIGHBORHOOD — DAY

Nice established neighborhood, older houses, mixture of residents— families with young children to retirees.

Yards and porches decorated for Halloween: scarecrows, carved pumpkins, ghost hangs from a tree, a cobwebby porch with giant spider.

MONTAGE OF NEIGHBORHOOD ACTIVITIES—

WOMAN sweeps porch.

MAN mows lawn.

DAD throws a baseball to SON.

KIDS on bicycles.

TEENAGER rakes lawn.

Down the street, moving van parked in street.

Furniture on lawn. TWO MEN move between van and house, loading the van.

END OF MONTAGUE

EXT. YARD - NEAR DUSK

Two men shutting van back doors. In driveway, a car sits loaded. Early trick-or-treaters go door-to-door.

Adult CHARLIE DICKENS, mid-30s, stands on sidewalk, clipboard thick with papers and color-coded dividers, watches men. Long day, men look weary. Charlie looks crisp and fresh from head to toe.

CHARLIE
We'll see you in two days.

He refers to the clipboard.

O.S. Van doors SHUT.

CHARLIE
A.M. sharp.

Van pulls away from curb.

Charlie flips another page, looks up, starts running after the van.

CHARLIE
Wait! You didn't sign my inventory list.

Van continues on. Charlie walks back to house.

Ten-year-old LINDY DICKENS sits on the top step, elbows on her knees, chin in hands. Wears jeans, sneakers, T-shirt, oversized jean jacket. Grumpy/sad face.

CHARLIE
Ready?

LINDY
I'm not moving.

Charlie looks at his watch. Looks down the road after the van. Looks at his watch again, anxious, then at Lindy again.

LINDY
I'm not leaving my friends. It's not fair.

His shoulders sag. He's been down this road before.

He sits beside her.

LINDY
Why did Mom have to die?

CHARLIE
She was sick, Honey.

LINDY
So why can't we stay here?

CHARLIE
Because I have a new job.

LINDY
But why the principal of my school? I'll never have any friends.

CHARLIE

We talked about this and decided this together. Change is good for the soul.

LINDY

You sound like a greeting card.

CHARLIE

That's what Mom always said.

Lindy leans toward Charlie, rests her head against his shoulder.

LINDY

I miss her.

Charlie wraps an arm around her and hugs her.

CHARLIE

I know. I do too.

Charlie stands, offers his hand.

Lindy looks at his hand, sighs, then finally puts her hand in his, and rises. Charlie takes one step down, but Lindy stays put.

She lets go and goes into the now empty house. Charlie follows.

INT. HOUSE

Their FOOTSTEPS ECHO in the empty house. They reach the—

INT. KITCHEN

Lindy pauses at the island and runs her hand along the counter-top.

FLASHBACK — INT. KITCHEN — A YEAR AGO

Lindy, and her mother, JEAN enters kitchen, their arms full of groceries. Jean wears jean jacket.

CUT TO:

Lindy and Jean roll dough, cut out Halloween cookies, laughing, talking. Jean dots Lindy's nose with flour.

END FLASHBACK

Lindy sighs and leaves kitchen. Charlie lags behind at the door.

FLASHBACK — INT. KITCHEN — A YEAR AGO

Jean at sink, washes rolling pin and cookie sheets. Charlie comes up from behind, wraps his arms around her waist, then turns her around and kisses her. She smiles at him.

Her eyes turn sad, her smile falters.

> JEAN
> The doctor called today.

> CHARLIE
> And?
> (beat)
> How long?

> JEAN
> A month... six weeks. At best. There won't be...
> (her voice catches)
> ... another Christmas.

END FLASHBACK

Charlie turns off the lights.

> CHARLIE
> (whispers)
> You almost made it to Christmas last year, Jean.
> (beat)
> Almost.

EXT. HOUSE — FRONT DOOR

Charlie stands on the sidewalk... waiting.

Lindy's hand on the doorknob, she starts to shut the door, then stops.

Sticks her head inside.

INT. HOUSE

> LINDY
> (whispering)
> Bye house.
> (voice shaky)
> Bye Mom.

She shuts the door.

O.S. FOOTSTEPS across porch, down stairs. Car doors SLAM. Through the door window, the blurred image of the car as it backs out the drive, then down the road.

INT. CAR

Lindy looks back, her gaze fixed on the house.

Finally, the house and neighborhood disappear. One lone tear trickles down her cheek.

Only then does she face forward, wrapping the jacket tight around her.

Charlie watches her as he drives. He starts to open his mouth to say something, reconsiders. He puts a hand on her leg and pats it.

She stares out the side windows, tears flowing silently. Lindy puts her hand in his and clasps it. He squeezes and she squeezes back.

EXT. CAR

— leaving city limits, entering freeway.

> LINDY O.S.
> How much farther?

EXT. CAR — LATE NIGHT

— as it pulls into a Kentucky motel parking lot. Charlie carries a sleeping Lindy into the room.

INT. DINER — MORNING

Charlie has shed his jacket and warm clothing for lighter clothing. Lindy still wears jacket. Both study menu.

Waitress places two glasses of water on table.

> CHARLIE
> I'll have two eggs, scrambled, rye toast, lightly
> buttered, two strips of bacon, crisp, and grits.

Lindy slowly lowers her menu and peers at Charlie over the top, her face scrunched up.

> LINDY
> Grits?

> CHARLIE
> You'll learn to love them.

Lindy shudders violently.

> LINDY
> I don't think so.
>   (to the waitress)
> I'll have the Belgium waffle. Lots of whipped
> cream.

INT. DINER

The waitress sets down their food, Lindy's waffle buried under the whipped cream. Lindy is about to take a huge bite of whipped cream.

Charlie holds out a spoon loaded with grits.

> CHARLIE
> Try it.

> LINDY
> Do I look stupid? Never!

EXT. CAR — LATE AFTERNOON

They pass a WELCOME TO GEORGIA sign.

INT. CAR

> LINDY
> Why can't we live in a neat state like Florida?

> CHARLIE
> Georgia's a great state.

> LINDY
> Name one thing that's great about it.

> CHARLIE
> No more snow to shovel.

> LINDY
> No snow! Dad, I love the snow. What about
> my ice skates? What about Christmas?

> CHARLIE
> It occurs down here, too. And they have rinks.

> LINDY
> But no snow?! That's sacrilegious!

She pouts, and stares out the window, her chin in her hand.

> LINDY
> Georgia sucks.

EXT. CAR — DUSK

The car passes the MISTLETOE CITY LIMITS sign. Lindy perks up, cranes her neck around to see everything.

Typical small Southern town. Tall courthouse with columns in center of town.

Rustic downtown. Bank. Library. Old-time movie theater. Fire-station with several firefighters in folding chairs in semi-circle, some tipped back resting against building.

Charlie waves. They wave back.

                              LINDY
                    You know them?

                              CHARLIE
                    No. Everyone waves here. It's called Southern
                    hospitality.

                              LINDY
                    You used to live here?

                              CHARLIE
                    When I was a little boy. Moved away when I
                    was a nine.

Car goes through town, turns down side street. Charlie pulls into a driveway. Turns off the ignition.

                              CHARLIE
                    This is it. Our new house. What do you think?

Lindy gets out of car, looks at house, neighborhood, then at her dad.

                              LINDY
                    Ask me again after high school graduation.

EXT. HOUSE

Lindy and Charlie unpack car.

INT. LINDY'S BEDROOM — NIGHT

Closet light on, door open, bare except for a few hangers and fewer clothes.

Small pile of boxes in the corner near the closet. Jean jacket hangs on doorknob. Lindy opens a box.

Charlie walks by the room, clipboard in hand, glances in, and stops.

                    CHARLIE
          Why don't you wait to unpack until after the
          furniture arrives. It'll make arranging the
          furniture easier.

He goes to one of the color tabs, flips it up, tears out a page and holds it out to her.

                    CHARLIE (CONT'D)
          Here's a copy of how to best arrange the
          furniture in your room.

                    LINDY
               Okay.

She folds the box flaps down, takes the paper from him.

Charlie leaves.

Lindy listens, goes to the door, peers out.

Satisfied he's gone, she turns around, walks across the room.

Opens boxes until she finds small wastebasket, pulls it out. Dumps its contents—desk stuff—on the floor, walks it to opposite corner of the room, sets it down.

Returns to her corner, grabs dad's sheet of paper, wads it up, throws it as if a basketball.

Ball bounces off wall, lands in basket. Lindy raises arms straight up in the air.

                    LINDY
               Two points.
                    (cheering like a crowd)
               Yay!

She tears into boxes, pulling out more stuff.

INT. HALL — COUPLE HOURS LATER

Sleeping bag and pillow in hand, Charlie opens her door and steps into—

INT. LINDY'S BEDROOM

—and stares.

Posters, movie star photos adorn walls. Closet light is on, knick-knacks arranged on shelf.

Lindy, her back to a wall, sits on the floor.

Two empty boxes, turned up-side-down, serve as mini-tables. A picture of her mother, and a picture of the three of them sit on one box. A soda can and several candy bar wrappers sit on the other. She's writing a letter.

Floor littered with empty boxes and stuff with no home. Paper wads surround wastebasket.

                    LINDY
          Neat, huh?
               (Beat)

Charlie gives her the you've got to be kidding me look.

                    CHARLIE
          Not quite the word I would use.

He hands her the sleeping bag and pillow.

                    LINDY
          We don't have to go to a motel tonight?

                    CHARLIE
          No, but I'm sure I'll regret this.

She jumps up, gives him a hug, kisses him on the cheek.

                    CHARLIE
          Movers will be here at eight.

                    LINDY
          I'll be ready. I promise.

EXT. BACK YARD - NIGHT

Charlie steps outside, into the dark, where streetlights don't shine. Back yard butts up against trees. Further up the hill is a forest.

At the edge of the trees, a reindeer with large spread of antlers. One ear bent.

Charlie freezes and stares.

Eye contact made. Bently snorts, nods its head.

Charlie sucks in air, blinks, wipes his eyes, looks again.

Nothing there.

Charlie frowns, runs a hand through his hair, looks around. Laughs, shakes his head.

CHARLIE
You're losing it. Long day. Nothing more.

He turns, starts back. Stops, turns, and looks one last time.

INT. HOUSE — MORNING — FRONT DOOR ENTRY

Front door propped open. Moving van parked at curb, doors open, furniture on lawn.

MEN move furniture into the house. Other MEN come out empty-handed.

Charlie flips clipboard pages with each piece of furniture he sees. Directs men to its location.

TWO MEN on the way out, come up behind Charlie, observe him working the clipboard while they wait for clearance.

They exit.

EXT. HOUSE — PORCH

FIRST MAN
I've never seen anything like it.

SECOND MAN
Me either. And, I'm not telling the wife. Don't
want to give her any ideas.

FIRST MAN
No one would believe us.

INT. LINDY'S BEDROOM

Door opens. Two movers with bed.

INT. HALL - LOOKING IN LINDY'S BEDROOM

Lindy asleep in a mess.

She wakes, sits up, hair every which way.

FIRST MAN
Where do you want it?

INT. HOUSE - NIGHT

Charlie moves through rooms, clipboard in hand. Furniture in place, boxes stacked neatly against walls. Boxes clearly identified with a number and the appropriate room.

INT. HALL - LINDY'S BEDROOM

He knocks on door.

LINDY O.S.
Come in.

Charlie opens door. Unmade bed and dresser in place. Drawers open, clothes cover everything.

Lindy's sits in middle of bed, going through teen magazines.

CHARLIE
Ah... bedtime. Big day tomorrow.

LINDY
Any chance you can have a different job by
tomorrow morning?

CHARLIE

Sorry.

LINDY

Because of you, I'm not going to have any
friends. When I grow up, all demented and
strange, it'll be your fault.

CHARLIE

Too late. Damage already done.

INT. HOUSE — MORNING

Charlie stands at the bottom of the stairs and shouts up.

CHARLIE

Come on, Lindy. Don't make us late.

Lindy races down stairs, wearing much the same outfit as before.

LINDY

Oh darn, not like you can send me to the
principal's office, now, can you?

CHARLIE

It's bad enough we're starting mid-semester.

LINDY

I hate being a new student.

CHARLIE

I was a new student lots of times. I turned out
all right.

LINDY

Says you.

EXT. MIDDLE SCHOOL PARKING LOT — MORNING

Charlie pulls into parking lot, parks car. Bell rings. Kids unload from buses and cars,
parents dropping kids off.

INT. SCHOOL OFFICE

Lindy and Charlie enter. Secretary, ANNIE BROOKS, typing, looks up. Middle-aged, no-nonsense, friendly, able to get a lot done in a short time. Peers over the top of her glasses.

                    ANNIE
          May I help you?

                    CHARLIE
          I'm Charlie Dickens.

Annie gets up and comes around the desk. Shakes his hand.

                    ANNIE
          Good to meet you, Mr. Dickens.
                    (looks at Lindy)
          And, you too, Lindy.
                    (to Charlie)
          I heard you were perfect for the job. Mr.
          Hadley dying the first day of school the way he
          did, heart attack, face down, right into his
          lunch. Spaghetti day. What a mess. Good to
          have a permanent prinicpal again, not like the
          other three who quit aft—
                    (to Lindy)
          Call me Miss Annie. Everyone does. I bet
          you're anxious to get to class.
                    (to girl walking past office)
          Donna?

DONNA, a student, comes into office.

                    DONNA
          Yes ma'am?

                    ANNIE
          Take Lindy to Miss Jacobs' room. She's
          expecting Lindy.

CHARLIE
(to Lindy)
See you after school.

Lindy looks like she's being dragged off to a torture chamber. The two girls disappear around the corner.

ANNIE
Don't worry, she'll be fine.

CHARLIE
Too many changes, I fear.

Annie leads Charlie into his office. Charlie follows.

ANNIE
Mr. Jeffers is still missing ten history books,
maintenance wants to change suppliers,
kitchen is complaining about the stove again,
students have started a petition. They want to
paint a mural in the cafeteria—

CHARLIE
Annie?

ANNIE
Yes, Sir?

CHARLIE
I need a clipboard. Any chance you have one?

INT. SCHOOL HALL

Bell rings. Charlie, clipboard in hand, stands outside the lunchroom, watches kids move past him. Notices one student, who's down the hall, approaching him.

CAROLE RINGER, same age as Charlie, looks much younger and like one of the students, hair in a ponytail, T-shirt, and pants. T-shirt has writing that can't be read, yet.

She interacts with everyone around her. Hi-fives one. Bumps hips with another. Gives a thumbs-up to a group of boys who all grin at her. She turns around, walks backwards for a step, turns forward, and pulls the braids of a girl in front of her.

Now close by, Charlie reads the T-shirt: *School lunches are cruel and unusual punishment.*

She passes him, her attention directed to student on her other side.

Charlie reads the back: *It's legal to hurl.*

He frowns.

A student taps him on the arm, distracting him, points down the hall. Two boys fighting.

Charlie races down the hall.

INT. SCHOOL LUNCHROOM — MINUTES LATER

Charlie returns to lunchroom and looks around. Not seeing Carole, he gets a tray and his lunch.

INT. TEACHER'S LOUNGE

Charlie opens door. Carole is there alone.

                    CHARLIE
          This room is for teachers only.

                    CAROLE
          That's nice.

Charlie sets his tray down.

                    CHARLIE
          I think—

                    CAROLE
          — that you have no idea who I am.

She sticks out her hand.

CAROLE
I'm the music teacher. Carole Ringer.

CHARLIE
Ah, the teacher who was out for gall bladder
surgery, wasn't it?

CAROLE
Yes. Feeling okay now.
          (beat - then smiles)
You don't remember me, do you? Of course
not. Ringer was my married name. I used to
be—

Charlie frowns.

CHARLIE
You look familiar.

CAROLE
It's been a couple decades.

CHARLIE
(sudden recognition)
Carole Cullen!

CAROLE
Ringer now.

CHARLIE
I wish I could say you haven't changed—

CAROLE
We both have.

CHARLIE
You never moved away?

CAROLE
No. Though, I left long enough to go to college.

Married a local boy, and I have a daughter.
You?

CHARLIE
Went to college, got married, and I have a
daughter, too. She's here wishing I wasn't.

CAROLE
Understandable.

Other teachers file in, sit down at the table, engaging both in conversation.

Both Carole and Charlie are aware of each other but no more opportunities for private
conversation.

INT. HOUSE — KITCHEN — NIGHT

Charlie and Lindy fix dinner. She cuts vegetables for a salad. He's at the stove, stirring.

LINDY
Why did you set up this kitchen like our old
one?

CHARLIE
Habit, I guess. It worked before.

LINDY
What happened to "change is good for the
soul?"

CHARLIE
This is about food preparation. Change in the
kitchen can cause indigestion. Besides your
method doesn't work.

LINDY
Says you?

CHARLIE
I saw your room.

                    LINDY
          It's better.
                    (beat)
          I met a girl in school today. She asked if I could
          spend Friday night with her. We're going to
          the movies.

Charlie opens his mouth to respond.

                    LINDY
          Don't get all dad on me. I need a friend.

Charlie observes her bent head, her focus on cutting. His shoulders drop.

                    CHARLIE
          Okay, but only after I get to meet her parents.

                    LINDY
          You already have and it's just her mom. She's
          the music teacher.

                    CHARLIE
          Carol Cul... er, Ringer?

                    LINDY
          Yeah, Rainy's parents are divorced.
                    (beat)
          Does this mean I can go?

                    CHARLIE
          Only if you do dishes tonight.

                    LINDY
          Deal!

INT. SCHOOL OUTER OFFICE — COUPLE DAYS LATER — MORNING

Annie glances up from her work. Looks to Charlie's office through glass. Door closed.
Charlie on phone. BOY sits in chair opposite Charlie.

Charlie hangs up phone, leans back in chair, studies boy. Finally, Charlie moves forward, talking. Boy nods. Charlie speaks again, boy nods again, this time hanging his head. Boy gets up, opens door, walks out, leaving door open. Annie watches as the boy leaves the front office.

Charlie gets up, watching, comes to Annie's desk.

> ANNIE
>
> He's a smart boy.

> CHARLIE
>
> Brilliant. Good grades, great potential, but his choice of friends—

> ANNIE
>
> He'll come around. His brother did.

Carole enters outer office, heads for mailboxes.

> CAROLE
>
> How's it going, Annie?

> ANNIE
>
> Double s, double gd.

Noticing Charlie's puzzled look—

> ANNIE
>
> Same stuff, different groundhog-type day.
> (to Carole)
> How are the auditions going?
> (to Charlie)
> Carole directs the Christmas pageant every year.

Carole retrieves her mail, sorts through it.

> CAROLE
>
> Today's the last day. In a few hours, I'll have my leads.

                         CHARLIE
          Lindy told me she's going to try out for the
          lead.

                         CAROLE
          You sound surprised.

                         CHARLIE
          I am. Though nothing she does these days fails
          to surprise me.

Annie and Carole grin at each other.

                         ANNIE
                    (to Charlie)
          Your roller coaster ride has just begun.

                         CAROLE
          Don't work too hard, Annie.

                         CHARLIE
          What about me?

                         CAROLE
          You're the principal. It's expected.

Carole leaves and Annie hauls out of her desk a foot-high stack of files and plops them
on her desk.

                         ANNIE
          Ready?

Charlie looks at the stack, sighs, pulls up a chair opposite her desk, and grabs the first
file.

INT. SCHOOL — OUTER OFFICE — LATER

Charlie hands Annie the last file.

                         CHARLIE
          All done. Thanks, Annie. Don't know how this

office would manage without you.

ANNIE
No worries. I have a contract with the devil.

Charlie laughs. Last bell of day rings.

INT. SCHOOL HALL

Students pour into hall, lockers open and close, kids leave the building, climb into buses and cars.

INT. SCHOOL — OUTER OFFICE

Through the window, as last bus leaves, a car pulls up. RON SMITH exits, walks into building, into outer office.

Annie places stack of papers in drawer, clearing off desk. Pulls purse out of a drawer.

ANNIE
Ron. What a surprise. Business or pleasure?

Charlie comes out of his office.

RON
A little of both.

Ron extends his hand. Charlie shakes his hand.

CHARLIE
Good to finally meet you in person.

Annie shoulders her purse.

ANNIE
If you two don't need me, I'll see you
tomorrow. Good-night.

CHARLIE
Good-night.

Annie leaves.

                    RON
Good-night.
          (to Charlie)
So, is everything going well?

                  CHARLIE
As well as can be expected considering how
things change from hour to hour.

                    RON
Have to tell you again how impressed the
other school board members and I were with
your credentials. You're a man who gets things
done.

                  CHARLIE
          (wry smile)
I try to. Part of the job description.

                    RON
What happened before doesn't matter to us.

                  CHARLIE
Why do I get the feeling this is more about
business than pleasure?

                    RON
We had an emergency meeting last night.
About finances. Our mileage request failed
recently.

                  CHARLIE
A problem lots of schools are having.

                    RON
We're asking each principal to cut his budget
by twenty percent, effective immediately.

CHARLIE

You're kidding.
(beat)
You're not. That's huge.

RON

And you're at a disadvantage. You haven't
been here long. Take my advice. Start with the
arts and ax the pageant. Cut anything that
doesn't deal with the basics.

CHARLIE

I'll need to study my budget.

RON

Understood. Wouldn't want you to do
otherwise. Don't cut any of the sports, though.
Can't have the students or their parents
protesting.

CHARLIE

They won't protest cutting the arts or the
pageant?

RON

Just a small number of people. They'll get over
it.

CHARLIE

What about the staff? Surely, we're not firing
staff this close to the holidays.
(frowns)
Is that why the other three before me left?

RON

Look at the budget and get back to me.
(shakes Charlie's hand and walks to the door)
I know you won't disappoint us.

INT. SCHOOL AUDITORIUM

Charlie enters.

Carole sits two-thirds of way down, watching kids onstage.

Some KIDS work on scenery. Other KIDS, as carolers, sing softly in the b.g.

As Charlie walks down the aisle toward Carole, one boy, TOM, in the middle of the stage, reads from script, interacting with another STUDENT portraying his friend.

> TOM
> Merry is driving me crazy! She thinks she's one
> of Santa's personal elves. If you ask me,
> Christmas is a season for greedy merchants—

Charlie steps slow, then stops, and he mouths the words silently as Tom continues.

> TOM
> — suppliers, bell ringers, tree growers. The
> only magic I see is how quickly the coin in my
> purse disappears.

Tom pulls out the empty pocket linings. Charlie mimics the action without actually pulling out the lining of his pockets.

> TOM
> How is there magic in this?

FLASHBACK — INT. SCHOOL AUDITORIUM

Young Charlie is on stage reading from the script.

> YOUNG CHARLIE
> (obviously nervous)
> And all that Fa-la-la-la-la-ing. It's driving me—

The DIRECTOR, who sits several rows back, interrupts.

> DIRECTOR
> That's fine Charlie.

Young Charlie stops, surprised he's been halted mid-sentence. He struggles to conceal disappointment.

INT. BACKSTAGE WING

He walks past where Young Carole stands, script in hand, ready to go on stage.

> YOUNG CAROLE
> I know you got the part.

> YOUNG CHARLIE
> (stopping)
> No, I didn't. I was horrible. It's just a dumb
> play.

Head down, Charlie runs to the stage door, bangs it open, lets it slam against the wall. Leaves.

INT. SCHOOL HALLWAY

Charlie kicks a locker, jams hands into pockets, walks to main entrance, leaves the building.

END FLASHBACK

Somebody throws a paper wad at Tom and it hits him in the head. He stops reading and reacts, bats away paper, looks around for the guilty party.

> CAROLE
> Okay, everyone. That's all for tonight. See you
> on Monday.

Some kids head backstage, some jump off the stage. Say good-night to both Carole and Charlie as they pass by.

Lindy, bubbly and bouncing, hugs her dad tightly. RAINEY RINGER is with her.

> LINDY
> I got the part, Dad! I'm Merry! Isn't it great!?

Charlie looks to Carole who smiles at Lindy.

CAROLE

She's a natural.

Unaware that Charlie isn't talking, Lindy continues.

LINDY

Are you ready to go?

CHARLIE

Hi, Rainey.
(to Lindy)
In a minute. Go on ahead. I'll meet you at the
car.

LINDY

Is it all right if Rainey spends the night with
us?
(to Carole)
Miss Carole?

The two adults exchange glances. Charlie hesitates.

CAROLE

Sure you wouldn't rather spend the night at
our house?

LINDY

I want to show Rainey my room.

She looks expectantly at Charlie.

LINDY

Dad?

CHARLIE

Sure.

CAROLE

I'll drop a bag off for Rainey later.

LINDY
Thanks, Dad. Thanks, Miss Carole.

RAINEY
Thanks, Mom.

The girls run off, heads together, giggling.

CHARLIE
How did that happen?

CAROLE
You said yes.

Carole gets up. Front of her shirt reads: *Feed on Literature.*

CHARLIE
No, her getting the lead.

Carole turns her back to him and picks up her books. Back of shirt reads: *Take a Book to Lunch.*

CAROLE
Pure talent.

CHARLIE
How does major procrastination and the
inability to clean her room turn into talent?

CAROLE
(laughing)
You too?
(all teacher again)
You really don't know, do you? Lindy's voice is
incredible. I told her she needs to join the choir.

CHARLIE
I've never heard her sing.
(beat)
I noticed it's the same play. And on Christmas

Eve?

CAROLE

It's tradition. I tried changing it when I first
started teaching, but no one would hear of it.
Or, my trying to move it to the last day of
school before vacation. Even though we use
the same play, each year it's different. Last year
the props fell. The year before, someone mixed
glue with the fairy dust and it came out of the
bucket in a blob.

Charlie stares at the stage.

CAROLE

Brings back memories, doesn't it?

Charlie turns away from the stage.

CHARLIE

Not a bit.

ELIZABETH, a student, interrupts them. She holds a music book.

ELIZABETH

Ms. Ringer?

CAROLE

Oh, Elizabeth, I forgot. I was going to help you
with your scales. Are you ready?

ELIZABETH

Yes ma'am.

CAROLE
(to Charlie)
Was there anything else?

CHARLIE

Ah... Nothing that can't wait a day or two.

INT. CHARLIE'S LIVING ROOM — NIGHT

The girls wear boxer shorts, T-shirts, socks, no shoes, feet on coffee table, consuming popcorn, drinking sodas. Wide-eyed, staring at TV, watching horror movie. As MUSIC CRESCENDOS eyes get larger.

Charlie walks into the room behind them. They don't notice.

>   CHARLIE
>   'Night, girls.

They scream. Popcorn flies.

Charlie grins, heads for the stairs.

>   LINDY
>   'Night, Dad.

>   RAINEY
>   Good-night, Mr. Dickens.

Rainey makes sure Charlie is gone.

>   RAINEY
>   Your dad is so cool.

>   LINDY
>   That's because you don't live with him.

>   RAINEY
>   I miss having Dad around.

Lindy clicks the TV off. Rainey picks up a photo album, thumbs through it as they talk.

>   LINDY
>   I miss having Mom around. Where is your
>   dad?

>   RAINEY
>   California. He's got a new wife and baby. We
>   don't get along.

LINDY
You and your dad?

RAINEY
No. His new wife. She hates me.

Rainey's eyes widen. She points to a young boy in a photo who stands next to a young girl, their arms around each other's shoulders, big grins on their faces.

RAINEY
Who's this?

Lindy looks.

LINDY
Dad. Why?

RAINEY
That's my mom with him.

Lindy's eyes widen. She grabs the album for a better look.

LINDY
What?! They knew each other?

RAINEY
Looks like. Think they were best friends?

LINDY
Are they still friends?

RAINEY
I don't know.

They grin at each other.

LINDY
Are you thinking—

RAINEY
— What you're thinking?

They do a pinkie grab, grinning even more.

INT. CHARLIE'S BEDROOM

Charlie grabs his briefcase that sits on chest at the foot of his bed and plops it on bed. Opens it. Takes out thick set of files and equally thick school clipboard thick with papers.

INT. CHARLIE'S BEDROOM — MUCH LATER

With pillows against his back, legs stretched out, Charlie sits on top of the bedspread, papers everywhere but in neat orderly piles.

With a disgusted sigh, he shuts the budget file he's looking at, tosses it on top of the bed, not caring how it lands.

He paces across the room, a hand through his hair. He stops. Hears the girls traipse by his room, GIGGLING. He smiles at the sound.

When he stares back at the bed, the smile disappears. He moves to the bed with renewed determination.

EXT. HOUSE — FRONT DOOR — LATE MORNING

Charlie opens the door and finds Carole on the doorstep.

CHARLIE
Come on in.

He opens the door wider. Carole enters.

INT. HOUSE

Charlie leads the way into—

INT. KITCHEN

CHARLIE
Coffee?

Carole nods.

                    CAROLE
          I take it the girls aren't up yet?

                    CHARLIE
          I think they pulled an all-nighter.

                    CAROLE
          Looks like you pulled one too.

                    CHARLIE
          We need to talk.

INT. KITCHEN

Carole sits at the table. Charlie pours two cups, takes them to the table. Sets them down, sits, pushes the sugar bowl toward Carole. She dips her spoon into the sugar.

                    CHARLIE
          Ron Smith came to see me yesterday. Just
          before I came to the auditorium.

Beat. Her hand pauses.

She continues spooning the sugar.

                    CAROLE
          He's using you.

                    CHARLIE
          You know, don't you? About the cuts.

                    CAROLE
          I've heard rumors.

                    CHARLIE
          You knew and gave Lindy the lead knowing
          there won't be a pageant.

                    CAROLE
          I know nothing of the sort. I told you, I heard
          rumors. I don't act on rumors. Never have.

CAROLE (CONT'D)
Don't let them use you.

CHARLIE
Who? The Board? I don't have a choice.

CAROLE
Narrow minds have been ruling this town far
too long.

CHARLIE
You think I like doing this?

CAROLE
Then don't.

CHARLIE
I don't have a choice.

CAROLE
(frowns)
Yes, you do. Find an alternative. How do you
not have a choice?
(beat)
You fire me, I'll haunt the halls. Don't do it,
Charlie. Those kids thrive working on that
pageant. For some, it's the only real family they
have at Christmas time. You take away their
creativity, you take away their spirit. You want
to be responsible for that? You know better
than anyone how important that pageant is.

CHARLIE

Carole—

Carole gets up, gathering her purse.

CAROLE
There's nothing you can say to change my

mind, Charlie. You want to cancel the pageant
you'll have to go through me to do it. Lindy
didn't get the part because I thought it would
stop you from canceling the pageant. She
earned the part.

From the doorway—

> LINDY
> (puzzled)
> Dad? Miss Carole?

Both Carole and Charlie startle and turn. Lindy in the doorway.

> CAROLE
> (to Lindy)
> I'm sorry, Lindy.
> (puts a hand on Lindy's cheek)
> Tell Rainey I'll pick her up in a couple hours.

Carole leaves. O.S. front door CLOSES.

> LINDY
> Dad? What did she mean about the pageant
> being cancelled?

INT. LINDY'S BEDROOM

Lindy storms into her bedroom. Slams the door.

Rainey on bed, reading, stops, sits up.

> RAINEY
> What is it?

> LINDY
> The Board wants Dad to get rid of the pageant!

> RAINEY
> What?!?

LINDY

Orders.

RAINEY

He wouldn't do that.
(beat)
Would he?

INT. SCHOOL OFFICE

Charlie's desk is amassed with papers spread out. Shirt sleeves rolled up. Sits in chair, tilts back, sheet of paper in his hands hides his face.

Annie, typing, looks his way.

Carole enters, waves a greeting to Annie, knocks on Charlie's door frame. Charlie lowers the paper.

CAROLE

Annie told me you're trying to find a solution
to the budget problem.

CHARLIE

I have a soft spot for my daughter.

CAROLE

I wouldn't like you if you didn't.
(beat)
Which brings me to the reason I'm here.
Tomorrow is Thanksgiving. Rainey and I
would like you and Lindy to come have dinner
with us.

CHARLIE

Feeling sorry for us because we have no other
family here? Or is this to make up for stomping
out of my house the other day.

CAROLE

Neither. I hate left-over turkey.

INT. CAROLE'S KITCHEN — THANKSGIVING DAY

Kitchen a disaster. Meal over, everyone helps with clean-up.

Dog, BENNY, eats leftovers from a plate on floor.

Benny finishes, Rainey picks up plate, puts it in dishwasher.

Carole, with plastic container in hand, goes to an overhead cupboard and sets the container on the counter. The way she plants herself in position catches Charlie's attention.

He stops wiping the dish in his hands and watches. Carole opens cupboard and plays catch with numerous plastic containers that spill out.

Spillage over, Carole re-stacks everything, inserts stack into cupboard, shuts the door quickly.

Turns around. Stops. Sees Charlie watching.

                    CAROLE
          What?

                    CHARLIE
          That's frightening.

                    RAINEY
               (grinning)
          That's nothing. You should see her medicine
          cabinet.

                    CHARLIE
          Please. I just ate.
               (to Carole)
          You need to get organized.

                    CAROLE
          And you need to get unorganized. I found
          something you might like to see. Old movies.

LINDY

How old?

RAINEY

When you and Mr. Dickens were kids?

CAROLE

(laughing)

Yes. Go set up the TV. We'll finish in here.

The girls leave the kitchen.

CHARLIE

Thanks for inviting us over. I wasn't sure how Lindy would handle the holiday. Last Thanksgiving was rough with Jean in the hospital. The first Christmas without her mom. We ended up at a Chinese restaurant. Only thing open.

Carole frowns.

CHARLIE

(seeing the frown)

She didn't want us cooking dinner. Too many memories. We skipped almost everything.

CAROLE

She's doing fine. There'll probably be moments, but being in a new place helps. You know kids and Christmas.

Charlie frowns. Carole notices.

CAROLE

She seems excited about Christmas.

CHARLIE

Her mother's doing. Filled it with magic.

He sneers slightly at that last word.

> CAROLE
> (frowns and probes)
> What about you?

> CHARLIE
> Girls are calling us!

He leaves.

Carole looks after him, wondering.

INT. CAROLE'S LIVING ROOM — DAY

Shades are drawn, room dark. Carole goes to cabinet and finds DVD and slides it in. Pushes *play*. On TV screen, a black and white movie. No sound.

Charlie and Carole as kids:

Riding bikes.

Flying kites.

Playing outside during a rain shower.

Two of them on stage. First, Carole doing a dance. Badly.

> CAROLE
> I knew I should have played the piano.

Rainey and Lindy laugh hysterically. Carole grimaces.

Then Charlie on stage, facing the audience, obviously reciting something.

> LINDY
> What are you saying, Dad?

> CHARLIE
> The Gettysburg Address.

RAINEY
Was this a talent show?

CAROLE
Yup. And your dad won, Lindy.

LINDY
(awed)
You're kidding?

CHARLIE
I still have the medal.

LINDY
Back it up. I want to see it again.

Carole does.

Charlie starts to recite the Address, his words matching young Charlie on screen, including emphasis to match arm/hand movements.

CHARLIE
...all men are created equal. Now that we are engaged in a great Civil War, testing whether that nation or any nation so conceived and so dictated can long endure. We are met on a great battlefield of that war. We here highly resolve that these dead shall not have died in vain. That this nation under God shall have a new birth of freedom and that the government of the people by the people for the people shall not perish from the earth.

The other three applaud.

CAROLE
Amazing talent.
(to Lindy)
Once your dad memorizes something, he never forgets it.

>   LINDY
> Don't I know it. Every time he mops the floors,
> he sings every floor cleaner jingle that's ever
> been on TV.

On screen, Carole and Charlie hold fishing poles. Each holds a fish, too. Charlie's is tiny, Carole's is huge.

More laughter.

Then Charlie and his father are on screen at the top of grassy hill, a sled with wheels.

>   LINDY
> Who's that?

Charlie stares at the screen.

>   CHARLIE
> My father.

On screen, Charlie gets on sled. His father gives him a push.

>   RAINEY
> Is that a sled? With wheels?

>   CAROLE
> We wanted snow in the worst way. Got a little
> that year. Didn't last long though... I remember
> your dad bought the sled then converted it for
> us, so we could use it without snow.

>   CHARLIE
> We signed our names on the bottom.
>   (beat)
> It was the last fun time I spent with Dad.

>   LINDY
> What happened?

Beat.

CHARLIE

He left us. On Thanksgiving.
    (beat)
I didn't know why right away, though. I
thought he'd gone on a business trip, as usual.
Later, I found he'd moved into an apartment.
Remarried and moved away the day after the
divorce. I never heard or saw him again.

LINDY

I didn't know that. Didn't he die before I was
born?

Charlie nods.

Rainey jumps up.

RAINEY

I'm ready for some pie. You want some, Lindy?

Lindy jumps up too.

LINDY

Sure.

RAINEY

Mom? Mr. Dickens?

CHARLIE

No, thanks.

CAROLE

Not right now, Sweetheart. Maybe later.

The girls gone, Carole looks at Charlie.

CAROLE

I didn't know all that. Is that why you and
your mom moved away? That must have been
rough.

                    CHARLIE
          I survived.

The video continues. Now it's the Christmas pageant.

One actor bumps into another and they both tumble. Carole and Charlie laugh.

The video ends suddenly.

                    CAROLE
          Remember how the director— what was his
          name?

                    CHARLIE
          Williams.

                    CAROLE
          How he nearly tore his hair out?

                    CHARLIE
          Served him right. He was awful.

Frowning, Carole looks at Charlie.

                    CAROLE
          You didn't think so in the beginning.
                    (beat)
          You're still upset you didn't get the lead.

Long beat.

                    CHARLIE
          I wanted to be the star.

                    CAROLE
          Why?

                    CHARLIE
          I thought Dad would come back and
          everything would be okay.

The two girls trail through the room, wearing lightweight jackets.

                    RAINEY
We're going outside for a while.

                    CAROLE
Don't go too far.

INT. CAROLE'S KITCHEN

Charlie and Carole sit, eating pumpkin pie a la mode.

Benny, the dog, sits on the floor between them moaning.

                    CHARLIE
What's wrong with Benny?

                    CAROLE
Ate too much turkey dinner like the rest of us,
didn't you, boy?
          (to Charlie)
Made a pig out of himself.

Carole offers Benny a bite of her pie and ice cream. Doesn't want to sniff it. Turns away.

                    CHARLIE
What happened to your marriage? I'm sorry.
Am I being too personal?

                    CAROLE
No, you're not. It wasn't meant to be. He was
second choice.

                    CHARLIE
What happened to your first choice?

                    CAROLE
I was still waiting to see how he turned out.

CHARLIE

How so?

CAROLE

I fell in love with him years before, but he
never really saw me.
(beat)
Trouble was Hank, my husband, knew he was
second choice from the beginning. We were
friends before we became lovers. At a low
point, he started remembering what I had told
him about being in love with this other guy.
His jealousy ate at him. Couldn't believe I
could love him too.

CHARLIE

Sorry to hear it.

CAROLE

Actually, it was my own fault that I'd settled.

Finished, Charlie takes his dish to the sink. Doesn't see Carole watching him.

CAROLE

How about you and your wife?

CHARLIE

I loved her. I liked being married.

He looks out the window: large yard, backed by tree line. Dusk. At the edge of the trees
is a reindeer. He frowns.

CHARLIE

(slowly)
But she always said I was holding back...

CAROLE

What do you think?

Charlie sees it move into the trees.

CHARLIE
(still looking out window.)
That it was her imagination.

EXT. YARD — NEAR DUSK

The girls enter the trees. Walking and talking.

EXT. AMONG TREES

Rainey stops puts a finger to her lip, then points ahead.

Lindy looks.

Ahead is a reindeer, antlers wide and heavy, one ear bent. He stands, stares at them.
Nods his head.

Behind the girls, BUSHES SHAKE. Startled, they turn. A crow flies out.

They look back at the reindeer. He's gone. A few snowflakes drift down. They look up.
A few more flakes and then, it stops.

RAINEY
(in awe)
Did you see that?

LINDY
Yeah, it was just a stupid old deer. I used to see
them all the time up where we lived.

RAINEY
The snow! And that wasn't just any deer. That
was the same reindeer Mom saw when she was
a little girl. The one she used to tell me about.
Bently's his name because of his ear. And it
snowed then, too.

LINDY
No way! Your mom and my dad are ancient.
Bently would be dead now.

                    RAINEY
I'm telling you, it's the same. Mom said he had
huge horns and a bent ear. His ear was bent.

                    LINDY
So what? What if it is Bently?

                    RAINEY
She said he has magical powers.

                    LINDY
No way.

                    RAINEY
Your dad's seen it too. That's what Mom said.

Lindy stares at her.

                    LINDY
Magic? And he's seen it?!?!

                    RAINEY
I wonder if we made a wish, if it would come
true.

They grin at each other.

INT. CAROLE'S KITCHEN

The girls crash through the back door.

                    RAINEY
Mom, you should have seen it!

                    LINDY
It was incredible!

                    CAROLE
Seen what?

RAINEY

Bently!

LINDY

The snow!

Charlie and Carole exchange a look.

Charlie looks out the window.

CHARLIE

Don't be ridiculous. There aren't any reindeer around here. We're too far south. And, there wasn't any snow. It's sixty degrees outside.

Rainey grabs Lindy's arm and pulls her out of the room.

RAINEY

Come on. Let's go upstairs. Maybe we can see it again from the window.

The girls leave the room.

CAROLE

You're denying what we saw that day?

CHARLIE

It was a white-tail deer, Carole. With antlers.

CAROLE

Antlers that don't look anything like regular deer.

CHARLIE

Don't tell me you still believe in that stupid magic thing we cooked up as kids?

CAROLE

You're holding something back.

Charlie glares, but only for a second. Now he looks haunted.

CHARLIE

I grew up.

CAROLE

Too bad we're not doing *A Christmas Carol*.
You'd make a perfect Scrooge.
>   (beat)
Just because your father said it wasn't a
reindeer, doesn't make it so. You saw it, he
didn't.

CHARLIE

Magic? It snowed because the conditions were
right. Period. It only lasted a few seconds, and
nobody else saw it snowing. Nobody. It was a
fluke.

CAROLE

It was special. Being a weatherman will be a
great fallback for you when the Board fires
you.

CHARLIE

Like the others?

CAROLE

No, they all quit. They didn't want to make a
difference.

Charlie face tightens.

CAROLE

>   (softly)
Sorry. That was uncalled for. But you saw
Lindy. She believes in the magic. Are you
going to take that away from her the way it
was taken away from you?

INT. GARAGE — NIGHT

Charlie, with Lindy in the car, pulls into the garage. Boxes stacked against back wall, along the sides, with an assortment of small furniture, lamps, and stuff.

> CHARLIE
> We need to clean out the garage.

> LINDY
> (groans)
> Do we have to? It's Thanksgiving vacation, not Thanksgiving jail time.

> CHARLIE
> I'll make a deal with you.

Lindy groans again.

> LINDY
> How come your deals are never any fun? Or in my favor?

> CHARLIE
> We spend tomorrow cleaning this out and the rest of the weekend is yours.

> LINDY
> Promise? Including a trip to the mall Saturday? Can we take Rainey?

> CHARLIE
> Promise. Though I'm sure I'm going to regret this, what with it being Thanksgiving weekend—

Lindy hugs him tight.

> LINDY
> The biggest shopping weekend of the year! I can't wait to see all the Christmas decorations!

CHARLIE
(groans)
What was I thinking?

INT. GARAGE — MORNING — NEXT DAY

Charlie and Lindy haul boxes to the curb and putting reusable stuff in the car.

LINDY
Why didn't we leave this stuff at the other
house if we're just going to donate it?

CHARLIE
Because I wasn't sure what we'd be using.
Besides, not all of this is ours. Someone left it
behind.

Lindy moves a couple boxes, pauses, sees something.

Quickly, she pushes stuff out of the way to get to it. She pulls out a sled. With wheels.

LINDY
Dad! Look!

Charlie looks. Frowns.

LINDY
It's your old sled.

CHARLIE
Don't be ridiculous. We got rid of that thing
years ago.

Lindy turns it over to see underneath.

CHARLIE
It can't be.

She hands it to him.

LINDY
The magic's still here, Dad!
I've got to call Rainey. She's not going to
believe this!

— and runs out of the garage. Charlie's in shock. Stares at the childish scrawls of two names: Charlie and Carole.

INT. MALL — FOOD COURT — NEXT DAY

Charlie and Carole sip soft drinks. One chair loaded with packages.

Carole's T-shirt reads *Kiss My Eraser* on the front. On the back: *Eat My Chalk Dust*.

CAROLE
You still don't want to believe in the magic, do
you?

CHARLIE
It's nothing more than a coincidence. We gave
that sled away. Somehow, it's gone through
multiple hands and ends up belonging to the
family whose house we happened to buy.
That's all.

CAROLE
How do you explain the shape it's in? Lindy
says it looks almost new.

CHARLIE
It didn't get used.

CAROLE
You have an answer for everything, don't you?

CHARLIE
Hardly. I'm still struggling over the budget.

CAROLE
Any luck?

(beat)
With no pageant December might as well cease
to exist.

CHARLIE
Works for me.

CAROLE
You hate Christmas that much?

Charlie looks off in the distance.

CHARLIE
I'm in unfamiliar territory. You're the expert—
(he waves he arm to include the mall)
— of all of this.

Carole laughs.

CAROLE
Thanks for toting my bags. I've made a great
start on my shopping list. But you haven't
bought a thing.

Beat.

CHARLIE
I almost wish someone would tear December
off the calendar. I'm not ready for this.
Christmas was Jean's holiday. It's just me and
Lindy now.

CAROLE
Jean's parents?

CHARLIE
Both gone. Years ago.

CAROLE
Sorry.

CHARLIE

Jean took care of everything. I don't have a clue
where to begin. Lindy's going to tell me what
she wants. She's making a list. Part of the
reason we're here today.

CAROLE

Uh-oh.

Carole spots Lindy and Rainey walking toward the table, talking, animated, loaded
with packages. They see Charlie and Carole and wave.

At the table, girls unload packages in empty chair.

Rainey picks up Carole's drink, takes a sip, replaces it in front of Carole. Carole picks it
up; it's empty.

Lindy hands Charlie a sheet of paper.

LINDY

Here's the first sheet, Dad. Rainey and I are
going to check out that part of the mall now.

She points to another wing of the mall.

Charlie looks stunned.

CHARLIE

First sheet?

Lindy grabs Rainey, drags her away. Instantly, they're swallowed up in the crowd.
Gone.

CHARLIE

What just happened?

Carole laughs.

CAROLE

And, just think. Soon, they'll be teenagers.

Charlie looks at the list, shock on his face. He shows it to Carole.

Carole's greatly amused.

> CHARLIE
>
> What do I do now?

> CAROLE
>
> First, we take this stuff to the car, and then we
> go shopping.

> CHARLIE
>
> (horrified)
> Tell me you're kidding? My feet hurt, I'm
> suffering from people overload, and those ho-
> ho-hos are beginning to grate on my nerves.

Carole laughs. Charlie sags.

> CHARLIE
>
> I knew there was a reason why I never went to
> the mall.

INT. INSIDE MALL STORE

Rainey and Lindy stand behind a shelf where they spy on their parents. Charlie struggles to carry several bags at once. One slips. Laughing, Carole re-adjusts it so Charlie can carry it.

> LINDY
>
> Neat idea you had with that long list.

> RAINEY
>
> Yeah, that should keep them busy together for
> a couple more hours.

> LINDY
>
> I don't want Dad to think I really want all that
> stuff, though.

RAINEY

Don't worry. Mom knows the top of the list is
the really important stuff. You'll see.

LINDY

Yeah. My mom was like that too. Now what do
we do?

RAINEY

Let's go try on wigs and Christmas hats.

EXT. TREE FARM FIELD — DAY — A WEEK LATER

Bright, sunny day. Girls and Carole dressed for the job: jeans, hiking shoes or sneakers,
T-shirts. Charlie is ready for the office. All that's missing is a tie and jacket.

Charlie and Carole tramp through the grass, heading for the pine trees in the distance
ahead. Rainey and Lindy romp ahead, throwing pine cones, giggling, chasing each
other.

Carole carries a small saw and a coiled rope over her shoulder.

CHARLIE
How did I let you talk me into this?

CAROLE
Because Christmas isn't Christmas unless
there's a tree in the house. Where else would
the presents go? Rainey and I do this every
year.

CHARLIE
I don't know—

CAROLE
You really are a Scrooge, aren't you?

CHARLIE
No!
(beat)

Not really.
> (beat)
Okay, so what if I am?

CAROLE
You're doing this for Lindy's sake.

He looks ahead at his daughter, at both girls.

CHARLIE
It's almost as if her mother never died, as if we never went through that dark time.

CAROLE
Children are resilient.
> (beat, looking pointedly at Charlie)
Most of the time.

Carole looks at Charlie from head to toe.

CAROLE
Seriously, that's your we're-going-to-be-hiking-through-the-woods outfit?

CHARLIE
When you said we were picking out a tree, I thought we were going to a tree lot.

Carole extends her arms to embrace the landscape.

CAROLE
We are!

As they talk and walk between the rows of trees. Carole inspects the trees.

CAROLE
It's all about the experience. This way, the tree hasn't been in the lot for days and days. It's fresh.

                    CHARLIE
So, pick one.

                    CAROLE
It has to be just right. Not too tall, too short, too
fat, too skinny.

                    CHARLIE
So, who's going to cut it down for us?

EXT. AT THE PERFECT TREE

Charlie kneels in the dirt at the base of a full, medium-sized tree not much taller than he
is, saw in hand.

                    CAROLE
Sure you don't want me to do that?

                    CHARLIE
And take me away from all this fun? How long
does it take to saw down one itty bitty tree,
anyway?

EXT. AT THE PERFECT TREE — MINUTES LATER

Charlie pauses, resting, wiping his forehead with the back of his hand, unaware he's
rubbing a streak of dirt across this face.

The sky turns cloudy. THUNDER.

EXT. AT THE PERFECT TREE — MORE MINUTES LATER

Downpour.

The two girls, holding hands, spin around in a circle, tongues out, faces toward the sky,
laugh, and lap up the raindrops.

Carole grins at them, looking skyward herself, enjoying the rain.

Looks to Charlie, who's muddy and grunts with every pull of the saw.

CAROLE

Let me saw for a while.

CHARLIE

Almost done. I want
          (grunt)
to enjoy this
          (grunt)
fun to the fullest. Only needs another
          (grunt)
saw or two.

CAROLE

No one asked you to do all the cutting.

Charlie pauses for a second, spots something in the distance, among the trees. He moves his head for a better look.

Bently stands facing Charlie. Then Bently's gone.

Charlie looks around. The girls throwing cones didn't notice. He glances at Carole.

She arches an eyebrow at him.

Frowning, he goes back to sawing.

The tree falls over.

Charlie stands, grimacing as he works out the kinks.

CHARLIE

Timber. Done.

CAROLE

I still think we ought to get your tree today, too.

CHARLIE

This is my tree.

Hands her the saw.

CHARLIE

Cut your own.

Carole laughs.

EXT. FIELD — DAY

Sun shining again.

Charlie drags one tree. Carole walks beside him. Girls drag another.

Everyone's soaked. Charlie a mess: pants black at the knees and his seat and hair has needles and twigs. Totally unkempt.

CAROLE

Seriously, I could have cut my own tree.

CHARLIE

And deprive you of my fun?

Laughter fills the woods.

INT. CAROLE'S UPSTAIRS HALLWAY — OUTSIDE BATHROOM DOOR

She opens the door a crack, holding out dry clothes.

CAROLE

Here you go, Charlie.

CHARLIE O.S.

Thanks.

Charlie's hand reaches out, grabs the clothes.

CAROLE

Give me your wet ones.

His hand reappears with wet clothes.

CAROLE

I'll put these in the washer. Come downstairs

when you're dressed. The girls are making hot
chocolate with heaps of miniature
marshmallows.

                    CHARLIE O.S.
Whose clothes are these?

                    CAROLE
The shirt's mine, the sweatpants belonged to
my ex-husband. Why?

                    CHARLIE O.S.
Isn't there anything else I could wear?

                    CAROLE
Not big enough to fit you.

A groan from the bathroom.

Carole walks away grinning.

INT. CAROLE'S KITCHEN

Girls at stove, talk, and take turns stirring hot chocolate.

Carole gets cups out of the cupboard, sets them on counter.

Charlie walks in room.

All three stop and stare.

They try not to laugh, try to maintain serious expressions.

Charlie's T-shirt, while big on Carole is snug on him. Across his chest it says: *I love full moons*. The sweatpants are short.

                    CHARLIE
What?

                    LINDY
Nothing, Daddy.

RAINEY
You look good, Mr. Dickens.

CAROLE
Real good.

CHARLIE
What can I do to help?

CAROLE
There's some cookies in the cupboard behind
you.

Charlie turns. Back of shirt reads: *I like to howl*. Laughter fills the room.

INT. CAROLE'S LIVING ROOM — DAY

Tree stands in the corner. Two girls stringing lights.

Benny wears reindeer headband with horns. Watches them.

Carole pulls angel out of its box.

Charlie stands to one side, tilts his head.

CHARLIE
It's crooked.

Carole drags a footstool over to the tree.

CAROLE
I know.

Carole climbs the footstool, it teeters. Charlie steps forward, holds her still, his hands on her hips.

Girls exchange a knowing look. Carole tops the tree with angel. Climbs down and off footstool. They all admire the tree.

CHARLIE
It's still crooked. I'll straighten it.

All three turn and speak in unison.

                    CAROLE, RAINEY & LINDY
          No!

                    CAROLE
          That's part of the charm.

EXT. CAROLE'S KITCHEN

Carole, at sink, wipes counter. Dishes done.

House is quiet. Girls upstairs.

Charlie enters, wearing his own clothes again.

                    CAROLE
          Feeling better?

                    CHARLIE
          More normal at any rate.

                    CAROLE
          Want some more hot chocolate? There's just
          enough for two more mugs.

Charlie gets the mugs and Carole pours the drinks. They sit at the table.

Carole takes a sip, sets her mug down.

                    CAROLE
          I saw it too.

Charlie's hand pauses mid-air.

                    CHARLIE
          Saw what?

Charlie brings the cup to his mouth and drinks.

CAROLE
Wanna talk about it?

CHARLIE
It wasn't the same for you.

CAROLE
You're right. My wounds are different than
yours, but it helps to believe in something.
What do you believe in, Charlie?

CHARLIE
I don't know. That time heals all wounds?

CAROLE
Really? How about there's order to the
universe?

CHARLIE
If that were true, Lindy would still have her
mother.

CAROLE
Order around you is what you're able to attach
to your clipboard.

CHARLIE
It keeps me sane.

CAROLE
No, it keeps you from not feeling.

CHARLIE
You wouldn't say that if—

CAROLE
If what? If I hadn't lost my parents? I did. Two
years after you moved away. A horrible car
accident. I grew up in a foster home here.
(beat)

CAROLE (CONT'D)

If I hadn't felt deserted and forgotten? All kids feel that way, Charlie. Even those with both parents. You're not the only one who's suffered. Look at Lindy. She's laughing, enjoying life. She's lost her mother, but she hasn't lost faith in you. In Christmas. In love.
> (beat)

Love, Charlie. I believe in love.

CHARLIE

I can't do it again.

CAROLE

So you believe.

CHARLIE

I was lucky to have it once.

CAROLE

You think you're only entitled to love once in your lifetime?

CHARLIE

Don't you?

CAROLE

No.

CHARLIE

But you said you're still waiting. Holding out for your first love.

CAROLE

You're changing the subject. I loved Rainey's father until our separate baggage screwed it up.

                    CHARLIE
Just shows that love isn't a cure all to
everything.

                    CAROLE
Well, it is for me, and I'm not buying what
you're selling.

INT. DINER — NIGHT — A WEEK LATER

Christmas decorations everywhere. Diner crowded with shoppers with packages,
parents with children, workers done for the day.

Charlie and Lindy in a front booth eating dinner.

                    CHARLIE
How's your chicken?

                    LINDY
Okay, but not nearly as good as the one we
make.

She pushes her fork around on her plate.

                    LINDY
Dad, there's all kinds of rumors going around
school.

                    CHARLIE
You know how I feel about rumors.

                    LINDY
Are you going to cancel the pageant?

Beat.

                    CHARLIE
I don't want to.

                    LINDY
You're not answering my question.

CHARLIE
There's nothing to say.

LINDY
You're going to do it, aren't you? Stop the
pageant and fire people.

CHARLIE
Don't we have some more shopping to do?

Lindy drops her fork. It CLATTERS to her plate. She crosses her arms and stares at him.

Charlie sighs, pushes his plate back, and leans back against the bench.

He and Lindy overhear two men behind him talking. It's two members of the school
board, WALTER MASON and BILL WOOD.

Lindy frowns, puzzled. Charlie turns his head, listening.

WALTER
So far everyone's complying except Dickens.
He's too involved with that Ringer woman.

BILL
Ron told us not to push him.

WALTER
But the pageant is still going on. Ringer was in
the store tonight getting more paint for the
backdrops. Told me so herself.

BILL
Go easy. Ron said Dickens will do the right
thing.

Charlie leaps to his feet, surprising Lindy. He signals for her to stay put.

He moves a step or two until he's standing at the edge of the table of the two men.

CHARLIE

Evening Bill. Walter. Didn't realize we were
having a Board meeting tonight.

The two men look at each other uneasily.

BILL

We aren't.

CHARLIE

Doesn't sound that way to me.

WALTER

Eavesdropping?

CHARLIE

Couldn't help it. Especially when you're
talking about me.

Walter squirms a bit in his seat. Bill remains steadfast.

BILL

We're just concerned, particularly when we
hear the pageant is still on.

CHARLIE

I'm handling it. Goodnight, Gentlemen.

Charlie turns to his table. Lindy stares at him. He picks up their check.

CHARLIE
(to Lindy)
Ready?

She scoots out of the booth and waits while he pays the bill, looking toward the two
men, who are watching them.

CHARLIE

Don't stare.

He pockets the change. Turns her toward the door.

CHARLIE

Let's go.

EXT. DINER PARKING LOT

Lindy leans back against the car, head down, her arms crossed. Charlie stops in front of her. She looks up, tears welling.

LINDY

Do you believe Mom could come back as a spirit?

CHARLIE

I... I'm... Why?

LINDY

Cause I keep smelling her perfume.

CHARLIE

Charlie sniffs the air.

LINDY

Not now, but back in the restaurant, when you got up and talked to those guys.
(Wipes at her eyes.)
When Mom died last Christmas, I didn't think I could ever enjoy Christmas again, but I am.

CHARLIE

I'm glad.

LINDY

No, you're not. I know what all the other kids say— that there's no Santa. And I know what you think. You're wrong. All of you. There's something special about Christmas. Not to believe is like not believing in air. It's real, Daddy. All of it. You cancel the pageant and I'll hate you forever.

She gets in car. SLAMS door.

Charlie stands, stares, looks through the window at her. Emotions cross his face: anguish, despair, being backed into a corner.

INT. LINDY'S BEDROOM — NIGHT

Door is open. Lindy in pajamas. Headset on, listening to music. Doing homework.

Charlie walks by, backs up. Pauses in doorway, observing.

He steps into room.

Lindy sees him. Pulls headphones down, around her neck.

He stands there, uncomfortable, slides hands into his pockets.

> CHARLIE
> Lindy. About Christmas—

> LINDY
> Do you believe in rainbows?

He's perplexed at the swift change of topic.

> CHARLIE
> Of course.

> LINDY
> But why? Why do you believe in them?

> CHARLIE
> Because I can see them.

> LINDY
> But you can't grab them.

> CHARLIE
> No. It's light refraction. It's science.

LINDY

Funny. That's the way I feel about Christmas.

She puts the headphones back on, dismissing him.

Charlie stands there a few seconds, then leaves, quietly shutting the door behind him.

EXT. HALLWAY — LINDY'S BEDROOM

He takes a step, then stops. He looks at the door, continues on down to his bedroom, shaking his head.

INT. LINDY'S BEDROOM

Lindy stares at door. Her shoulders sag. Sad expression.

EXT. CHARLIE'S BACKYARD — NIGHT – LATER

Full moon. Dark house. Back door. Charlie exits in PJs and loose robe. Ties robe tight.

Steps out into the yard. Slides hands into pockets, shoulders hunched, head down.

RUSTLE OF BRANCHES. Charlie looks up.

Reindeer stands in front of him, about twenty feet away. They look like two contenders squaring off.

Reindeer snorts, stomps foot, shakes his head.

Charlie's face contorts in anger. He waves he arms.

CHARLIE

Get out of here!!!!

Reindeer holds his stance.

Finally shakes his head again, lowers it, BELLOWS. A wailful sound. Trots off into the woods. Disappears into the trees.

Charlie turns. Sees a face in the window. Lindy. Curtain drops.

INT. SCHOOL HALL

Empty halls. Bell RINGS. Doors open and kids fill the halls.

Rainey and Lindy meet up. Walk together to their lockers.

> LINDY
> I'm beginning to think it's a lost cause. Talk about cracking a hard nut. I think I'd rather try cracking a rock.

> RAINEY
> It'll happen. Adults are funny that way. You can win him over.

> LINDY
> With what? I'm out of four-leaf clovers and rabbits' feet.

> RAINEY
> You can't give up, Lindy. If you have any doubts at all, it won't work.
> (beat)
> He's a bad influence on you. Let's ask Mom if you can spend tonight night at my house. We've got to get you out there.

> LINDY
> But then Dad will be alone. A lot of good that does us.

> RAINEY
> (grinning)
> Don't worry, he won't be alone. I've got a plan.

INT. PIZZA HUT — NIGHT

Carole, Charlie, and the two girls enter.

Carole's T-shirt reads: *Music Teachers Are Noteworthy*

Shown to a table. The two girls quickly slide onto one bench together leaving the other side for Carole and Charlie.

Charlie lets Carole slide in first.

The girls grin at each other. Carole and Charlie observe the girls' grins.

As soon as their order is taken, the girls get up.

> RAINEY
> We're going to go say hi to Becky and Sara.

They leave, cross the room, settling into a booth with BECKY and SARA, school friends.

Charlie glances after the girls.

> CHARLIE
> This is beginning to look like a setup.

Carole laughs.

Charlie moves, as if he's going to get up and move to the other side. Carole puts a hand on his arm, stopping him.

> CAROLE
> Don't.

> CHARLIE
> Carole, we can't have the girls thinking their
> scheme is working.

> CAROLE
> Relax. I don't bite.

> CHARLIE
> Yes, you do. Remember that time —

> CAROLE
> That's because you called me a busybody.
> Nobody calls me a busybody.

Charlie laughs.

CUT TO:

— the other booth where Rainy and Lindy watch their parents.

> RAINEY
>
> Look, he's laughing.

> LINDY
>
> Think they know what we're doing?

> RAINEY
>
> Not a chance. I'm too good at this. I'm telling you, we're going to be sisters for real.

CUT TO:

— first booth.

Charlie notices Carole looking past him at the girls.

> CHARLIE
>
> What is it?

He starts to turn, to look.

> CAROLE
>
> No, don't look. I can tell from that expression on Rainey's face, she thinks she's successfully played matchmaker.

> CHARLIE
>
> She does this often?

> CAROLE
>
> Often enough. And with frightening results.
> (beat, looking at him)
> Not with me!

Charlie looks at her with renewed interest.

CHARLIE
What are you hiding?

Carole fidgets.

CAROLE
Nothing.

CHARLIE
Liar. You never could keep from telling me the truth, Bugs.

CAROLE
(surprised)
I'd forgotten that nickname.

CHARLIE
I hadn't. I doubt I'll ever forget the look on your face that time we found all those ladybugs in the forest.

CAROLE
It was a sight to see, wasn't it?

Charlie's face softens, remembering.

CHARLIE
(softly)
Yeah. It was something.

Charlie kisses her on the cheek.

CAROLE
What was that for?

CHARLIE
Thanks for being here.

CUT TO:

— other booth.

> RAINEY

Did you see that?

> LINDY

He kissed her!

They hi-five each other.

INT. CAROLE'S CLASSROOM — DAY

Carole conducts with her hands as class harmonizes a Christmas carol. Sees Charlie through the door window.

Carole pulls one child out of the lineup and has him conduct in her place.

She goes to—

INT. SCHOOL HALL

She shuts the door, frowns, seeing his expression.

> CAROLE

Something wrong?

> CHARLIE

Only if you say no. Go out with me tonight. It's Friday night, the girls can stay together.

> CAROLE

Is this a date?

> CHARLIE

Like last night? No. That was dinner. This is a distraction.

> CAROLE

As in tied up in knots over the budget?

> CHARLIE

How do—

CAROLE

Pick me up at seven.

She opens door, shuts it. Leaves him standing there alone.

INT. CAR — NIGHT

Charlie drives, grimly stares ahead. Carole observes him. She's wearing a Christmas sweater.

CAROLE

Has the fun, excuse me, the distraction part
started yet?

Beat.

CHARLIE

Not yet.

INT. MOVIE THEATER LOBBY

Charlie and Carole stand in line for popcorn and drinks. Poster of a classic Christmas movie is playing.

CAROLE

Has it started yet?

Beat.

CHARLIE

Not yet.

INT. DARKENED MOVIE THEATER

Their eyes glued to screen. Sharing large tub of popcorn. Hands reach into it at the same time.

They look at each other, smile. Looks linger. He becomes genuinely aware of her.

He leans toward her slightly, his expression changing. Someone bumps them from behind. They smile.

CHARLIE
Now it has.

INT. DINER — LATER

They share a huge hot fudge sundae.

CAROLE
I wouldn't have thought you were a hot fudge
sundae fan. Especially with peppermint ice
cream. Banana split, maybe. Peanut butter
flavored malt, for sure.

CHARLIE
Good, you're surprised.

CAROLE
Oh, it's okay for me to be surprised, but not
you?

CHARLIE
You're not wearing a cause on your chest
tonight. What happened?

Carole licks the fudge off spoon. Much like a kid would.

CAROLE
You're changing the subject.

CHARLIE
(laughing)
So did you.

Ron Smith and his WIFE and FAMILY enter diner.

Charlie and Carole spot him at the same time.

Immediately, their lighthearted mood evaporates. He pushes the sundae toward her.
Carole swirls her spoon in the cup.

CHARLIE

If I do my job, I lose my daughter. I do what's
right by Lindy, I lose my job.
(beat)
I need this job. I was fired from my last two
jobs because I was doing the right thing.

CAROLE

But, you got this job.

CHARLIE

They were desperate. They knew I was too.

CAROLE

There's got to be a way.

CHARLIE

You and I aren't alumni of the happy-endings
club.

CAROLE

We're still young.
(beat)
Aren't they concerned you've done nothing so
far?

CHARLIE

No doubt. Ron leaves me a voicemail at least
twice a week.

CAROLE

Which you never answer.

CHARLIE

How--?

CAROLE

Annie.

INT. SCHOOL — OUTER OFFICE — MONDAY MORNING

Charlie hands Annie an envelope.

> CHARLIE
> Annie, see that this gets delivered to Ron Smith
> today, please.

> ANNIE
> Sure thing.
> (beat)
> Any clues?

Charlie shakes his head and returns to his office.

INT. CHARLIE'S HOUSE FRONT DOOR — LATE AFTERNOON, SAME DAY

Lindy opens front door, a big smile on her face. Recognizes Bill, Walter, and Ron. Smile fades.

> RON
> Is your father home?

> LINDY
> I'll get him.

She turns. Takes a couple steps. Stops. Charlie is already there.

> CHARLIE
> (to the men)
> Would you like to come on in?

The three men stand uneasily, glance at each other, at Lindy.

> CHARLIE
> (to Lindy)
> Thanks, Honey. Run on up to your room now.

> LINDY
> (hesitantly)
> Sure, Dad.

She moves, but once out of sight of her father and the men. She lingers. Listening.

> RON
>
> We'd rather stay out here. What we have to say won't take long.

The three men back up until they're in the middle of the porch.

Charlie steps out, not quite shutting the door.

> WALTER
>
> We understand rehearsals are continuing. We thought—

Ron puts a hand out. Walter stops.

> RON
>
> I got your proposed budget cuts. It's not the twenty percent like I, we asked for. It's only twelve percent.

> CHARLIE
>
> Twenty is unreasonable.

> RON
>
> You're putting yourself in a dangerous position. If you don't do as you're asked—

> CHARLIE
>
> I'm working on it.

> RON
>
> No. You need to—

> CHARLIE
>
> I need more time.

> RON
>
> From where we stand, it looks like you're stalling.

                    BILL
It's more than your job at stake. It's your career.

                  CHARLIE
Is that a threat?

                    RON
No. A promise. We have the power.

The three men leave.

Charlie stands there. Watches them get into their car, his hands jammed into pockets, jaw hardened.

INT. HALLWAY

Charlie shuts the door. Turns, stops, sees Lindy.

                   LINDY
Don't let them bully you.

He opens his mouth to stay something, then stops. Finally —

                  CHARLIE
I don't have a choice.

                   LINDY
You know what? You're right. There's no
Santa. There's nothing. It doesn't matter
anymore. It's just a dumb old play.

She runs to her room.

O.S. door SLAMS.

He moves into —

INT. KITCHEN

Goes to the counter where there's a cutting board and partially cut vegetables.

He picks up knife. Hesitates. Abruptly slams the knife back down against the board.

His arms spread, he braces hands against the counter and hangs his head.

He raises his head and looks out the window.

Reindeer stands at the edge of the woods. It nods its head.

Angry, Charlie runs to the door, throws it open.

EXT. YARD

Outside, Charlie skids to a stop. Looks around.

His chest heaves. There's nothing. No one. No reindeer.

Charlie's all alone as he looks around.

EXT. SCHOOL PARKING LOT — NEXT DAY

Charlie pulls up. Hasn't even turned off car before Lindy is gone, slams door behind her.

Charlie sighs heavily.

INT. CHARLIE'S KITCHEN — NIGHT

Lindy cooking dinner. Puts lasagna into pot of boiling water.

Charlie enters.

CHARLIE
Want me to assemble everything?

Lindy stops what she's doing. Doesn't look at him and moves toward door.

LINDY
I have homework. Thanks.

She's gone before he can respond.

INT. CHARLIE'S KITCHEN — MINUTES LATER

A knock at the back door. It's Carole.

He lets her in.

> CAROLE
>
> I got your message.

Goes to covered pot on stove, lifts lid, view sink contents.

> CAROLE
>
> Lasagna, huh? You didn't tell me. We could
> have combined forces—

> CHARLIE
>
> Carole, sit down, please.

Surprised, she frowns at his serious tones and does.

> CAROLE
>
> What's wrong?

He starts and stops a couple times.

> CAROLE
>
> Spit it out. Is it us? The lasagna? What?

> CHARLIE
>
> I don't want to do this—

Beat.

> CAROLE
>
> Then don't.

> CHARLIE
>
> The pageant is cancelled.

> CAROLE
>
> No.

CHARLIE

And you're out of a job.

She stands, clearly agitated.

CAROLE

Just like that?
(beat)
I told you before, you aren't going to get rid of
me that easily. I'm staying whether I get paid
or not. These kids need me. They need the
pageant. Everyone benefits from it, except for
some Scrooge-like lost souls who year after
year are out to destroy it. Sounds like those
parents, those people finally got to the Board
and now you're going to be the Board's stooge
and do what they say. Look how it still affects
you and not in a good way!

CHARLIE

This isn't about me.

CAROLE

It's more about you than you know.
(beat.)
But you're not going to budge, are you?

CHARLIE

(in agony)
I can't.

CAROLE

The pageant's this Saturday, four days away.
You can't do this!

He doesn't respond.

She turns and goes toward the door. Grabbing the handle, she looks back.

CAROLE
You're right. You have changed. And I don't
like what I'm seeing.

Door closes behind her.

Charlie sighs, turns. Lindy is in the doorway.

Tears spill from her eyes, down her cheeks.

LINDY
Why? Why'd you do it? You didn't have to.

CHARLIE
I'd lose my job and we'd have to move again.

Lindy's shoulders shake. Charlie steps forward.

Lindy steps back, her jaw hard, her eyes like daggers.

LINDY
Don't touch me. I hate you!!!

She turns and runs out of the room.

O.S. FOOTSTEPS on stairs. Door SLAMS.

Pot boils over on stove. Charlie races toward it.

INT. CHARLIE'S KITCHEN — SOMETIME LATER

Charlie opens oven. Pulls out baked lasagna, places on table's hotplates that's set for
dinner.

He goes to the kitchen door and yells.

CHARLIE
Lindy. Dinner's ready!

He listens. Silence.

INT. HALLWAY

Charlie knocks on her door.

                    CHARLIE
          Lindy?

Silence.

He opens the door.

Empty room. Charlie checks behind the door, goes to the window and looks out.

INT. HALLWAY

He checks bathroom. Empty.

Opens any closed door in hallway. All empty.

Opens door to his bedroom—

INT. CHARLIE'S BEDROOM

Turns on light. In middle of bed is a note, propped against pillow.

Races to it, grabs, reads.

EXT. FRONT YARD

He shoots out the front door, yelling her name. Goes to curb, looks up and down street. Yells her name again. Nothing.

Races back inside.

INT. KITCHEN

Picks up phone. Dials.

                    CHARLIE
          Carole. Is Lindy there?

He looks up at ceiling. Grips phone.

CHARLIE

She's gone... she overhead us... Yes, she left a
note... No, you stay there. She may be heading
your way. I'll look for her... Yes, I'll call you the
minute I hear anything... Yes, call me if you
hear anything.

Pockets phone. Grabs a jacket, keys.

EXT. YARD — NIGHT

Crescent moon, lots of clouds. He circles yard, yelling her name again.

After each call, he listens, expecting... Just usual night noises.

INT. CAR

Drives down a deserted road, pines on both sides. Looks from one side to the other.

Glances ahead, jerks, brakes suddenly.

In his beams, Bently in middle of road. Facing him, not moving.

Charlie — gaze fastened on reindeer — gets out of car, moves in front of car and stares.
Takes a step forward. Bently bends his head down, rears head up, snorting. Stares at
Charlie.

CHARLIE

Where is she?

Bently repeats head move, snorts again.

CHARLIE

Where is she?!? I know you know.

Bently pauses, swings head to the left. Goes down road's gully and trots to edge of pine
forest.

Charlie watches.

Bently stops, looks back, moves into forest.

Charlie follows.

In the forest, difficult for Charlie to see Bently. Every time he thinks he's lost Bently, he sees him again.

Bently enters small clearing.

Charlie rushes up to it.

> CHARLIE
>
> Where is she?

> LINDY
>
> (faintly)
>
> Daddy?

Charlie turns to his left. Over by a fallen tree is Lindy. Curled up in a ball.

Charlie races to her. Gathers her up.

> CHARLIE
>
> Oh, Lindy. You scared me to death. I thought
> I'd lost you!

> LINDY
>
> It's my ankle. I think I twisted it.
> (Charlie looks at it)
> How'd you know where to find me?

Charlie looks behind him. Bently is gone.

> CHARLIE
>
> I got lucky.

With Lindy in his arms, he stands.

> CHARLIE
>
> We're going to the hospital.

INT. HOSPITAL — EMERGENCY ROOM

Charlie at the desk, filling out forms.

Carole races in through the doors.

                    CAROLE
          Where is she?

                    CHARLIE
          With the doctor. She's okay, just twisted her
          ankle. A little ice and some tape and she'll be
          fine. She's terrified that she can't be in the
          pageant.

Carole hugs him.

                    CAROLE
          Can I go see her?

O.S. Lindy calls out to Carole from behind an ER curtain.

Carole disappears behind the curtain.

INT. HOSPITAL — EMERGENCY ROOM

Charlie and DOCTOR shake hands. Lindy stands on one leg, next to Carole for support.
Injured foot, taped, lifted off floor.

                    DOCTOR
          Just make sure she stays off the foot tonight.
          Tomorrow it may still be a little tender, but I
          think the patient will live.
               (to Lindy)
          No more running through the woods in the
          dark, young lady. You were lucky this time. In
          fact, no running the rest of the week.

                    LINDY
          Yes, sir. I can still be in the pageant?

Doctor nods.

Linda smiles, hops a step forward. Charlie sweeps her up in his arms instead.

Carole opens the exit door.

EXT. HOSPITAL

At the car, Charlie deposits Lindy in the back seat, where she puts her foot up on the seat.

Charlie shuts the door. Turns to Carole.

> CHARLIE
> Thanks for being here.

> CAROLE
> I care about Lindy. Where else would I be?
> 'Night.

She turns, gets into her car, drives away.

Charlie goes around to his door. Hand on the handle, he looks up.

Bently stands at the edge of an otherwise nearly empty parking lot.

Bently nods its head, turns, trots away.

INT. LINDY'S BEDROOM

She's in PJs, in bed. Charlie tucks her blanket around her. Kisses her forehead. Starts to rise from her bed.

Lindy grabs his hand, stops him.

> LINDY
> I'm sorry for running away. I was angry.

> CHARLIE
> I know. I'm sorry, too. I know you're
> disappointed. In me. In everything.

                              LINDY
                    No more than you are.
                         (beat)
                    It's okay. Carole explained everything. 'Night,
                    Daddy.

She turns on her side. Closes her eyes.

Charlie frowns. Carole explained everything?

Charlie kisses her again.

                              CHARLIE
                    'Night, Baby.

He rises, moves across the room, turns out light, closes door leaving it open just a crack.

Looks into the darkened room.

O.S. Charlie's FOOTSTEPS fade away. A thin sliver of light shines into the room.

Lindy's lids open. She rolls onto her back, looks up at the ceiling, sits and looks out the window. She smiles.

EXT. BACK YARD — NIGHT

Charlie stands in middle of yard. Waiting....

Finally, wait is rewarded. Bently comes out of the woods, approaches Charlie. Slowly.

Charlie puts out a hand. Bently comes up to Charlie, huge antlers surround Charlie.

Charlie pets him.

                              CHARLIE
                    Thank you.

Bently backs away, turns, walks away. Disappears into forest again.

Charlie takes a deep breath. Looks up at the moon.

EXT. SCHOOL PARKING LOT — NEXT DAY

Charlie pulls into a parking space, turns off ignition. Lindy immediately has the door open.

                    CHARLIE
          Lindy, wait.

She waits but keeps her back to him.

                    CHARLIE
          Go to rehearsal tonight.

Lindy spins around, not sure she heard right.

                    CHARLIE
          Don't do something stupid like quitting.

                    LINDY
          I won't.
                    (beat)
          You know, Dad, just once I'd like to see you
          angry, normal like the rest of us. When Mom
          died, you didn't scream. You didn't cry. Least
          not that I knew of. I don't want to have to
          move again. I like it here.

Quickly she leaves.

Charlie continues to sit. Watches Lindy, animated, get absorbed into the crowd of students getting off buses, all headed for the school building.

Finally, last child is inside the school. Buses pull away.

Bell rings.

Charlie gets out of the car.

Slowly strides toward school.

INT. SCHOOL OFFICE

Annie looks up as Charlie enters. He's frowning and more focused than usual. Almost distracted.

> ANNIE
>
> Morning.

> CHARLIE
>
> Reschedule any appointments.

> ANNIE
>
> Yes, sir.

Turns to leave, then spins back around, briefcase in hand.

> CHARLIE
>
> We got any spare clipboards?

Annie gets up and goes to a cupboard.

> ANNIE
>
> How many do you want?

She opens the cupboard. Pile of new clipboards. Charlie takes one, kisses her on the cheek.

> CHARLIE
>
> Thanks.

She's caught off guard, her frown continues.

Phone rings. She answers, watching as he grabs papers from his briefcase and clips them to the board.

He leaves the office and out the building. He's forgotten his briefcase. Annie takes it to his office and puts it on his desk.

EXT. SCHOOL BUS GARAGE

Charlie parks his car. Walks toward garage.

Greets drivers, mechanics, shakes hands, with everyone he meets. Ignores any dirt or grease.

INT. SCHOOL BUS GARAGE

Semi-circle of people around Charlie: drivers, mechanics. They're doing all the talking. He listens, nods his head.

EXT. SCHOOL BUS GARAGE

Door wide open, most employees at the entrance. Charlie shakes hands. Gets into car, waves. They wave back. Happy faces.

EXT. ROADSIDE

Car parked off the road, out of sight of garage. Charlie sits writing notes. Finished, tosses clipboard onto passenger seat. Starts driving.

INT. RESTAURANT

Noon rush.

Charlie goes from table to table, introduces himself, shakes hands. Has clipboard tucked under his arm where it stays. He listens more than he talks.

EXT. RESTAURANT

Stops on sidewalk, writes notes on clipboard.

EXT. COURTHOUSE

Crosses street. Walks to entrance.

INT. COURTHOUSE — HALLWAY

Charlie goes to directory displayed in foyer. Fingers TAX ASSESSOR'S OFFICE on directory. Heads for it.

INT. TAX ASSESSOR'S OFFICE

Charlie talks with clerk.

She puts a big book in front of him. He goes through it, making notes.

INT. TAX ASSESSOR'S OFFICE — LATER

Charlie hands the clerk his notes.

She returns with copies of files requested. Hands them over.

INT. COURTHOUSE — HALLWAY

Charlie looks for another office. Finds it. CLERK OF COURT.

INT. CLERK OF COURT OFFICE

Looks through records, makes notes, requests records, makes copies.

EXT. CAR — COURTHOUSE PARKING LOT

Charlie clips papers to clipboard.

INT. SCHOOL OFFICE — LATE AFTERNOON

Annie gone. Halls empty.

MUSIC and VOICES come from the auditorium.

Charlie sits at his desk, going through papers, signing some, putting others aside, a serious expression on his face.

INT. SCHOOL HALLWAY

Carole leaves the auditorium, her jaw set, marches toward Charlie's office.

INT. SCHOOL OFFICE

Charlie looks up hearing footsteps in the office. He smiles seeing Carole. When she doesn't return his smile, his diminishes.

Carole enters inner office, shuts door.

CAROLE

I overhead Lindy telling Rainey you had some
visitors yesterday.

CHARLIE

Yes.

CAROLE

And?

CHARLIE

I was reminded to do my job.

CAROLE

And?

CHARLIE

I'm doing it. But not everyone is going to be
happy.

CAROLE

Don't you think everyone benefits from a
school play?

CHARLIE

Certainly.

Beat.

CAROLE

I have no idea who you are anymore. But, you
sure remind me of your—

CHARLIE

My father.
        (Carole is surprised)
Yeah, I'm surprised too.
        (beat)
I was thinking of quitting. Like he did with our
family.

CAROLE

What?! You can't quit! You can't let them chase
you out! What about the next guy? You think
he stands a chance doing any better than
you're doing right now?
(beat)
Wait a minute. Was?

CHARLIE

So far, I haven't done anything.

CAROLE

(thoughtfully)
Where were you all day?

CHARLIE

Go out with me tonight.

CAROLE

Another distraction?

He nods. His phone rings. He looks at caller ID and shuts it off, pocketing it.

CAROLE

Wrong number?

CHARLIE

Something like that. Which movie do you want
to see?

INT. SCHOOL AUDITORIUM — CHRISTMAS EVE NIGHT

It's Christmas Eve and the night of the pageant. Charlie goes backstage.

INT. SCHOOL AUDITORIUM — BACKSTAGE

Curtain closed. Kids move back and forth on stage. Charlie peeks through the curtains
and sees parents and family filling up the auditorium.

SEVERAL KIDS adjust props.

OTHERS KIDS pace from nerves.

TWO KIDS rehearse their lines with each other, interacting.

Lindy sees her father, gives him a thumbs up.

Charlie peeks through curtain again, sees Ron and other board members stride through auditorium up to the stage quickly, and turn toward the stairs leading backstage.

Charlie meets them at the top of the stairs.

> CHARLIE
> Gentlemen. Thanks for coming to the pageant.

> RON
> That's not—

> CHARLIE
> In my office.

Not waiting for an answer, Charlie leads the way. The men hesitate, then follow.

INT. SCHOOL OFFICE

Everyone in the office, Charlie shuts the door.

Through the glass, parents and kids move toward the auditorium. Some wave.

Charlie waves back, then turns his back on the window.

> CHARLIE
> I'll get right to the point. The pageant is on. My
> decision.

> RON
> Then you're fired.

> CHARLIE
> Not yet I'm not. Read my contract. The only
> way I can be terminated is a result of a board
> meeting.

WALTER
We're having a meeting now. I second it.

Charlie shakes his head.

CHARLIE
Again, read my contract. You have to fire me in
writing and I get a six-month's salary
severance pay. Not a great way to save money
in my mind. I wonder how the community
would feel about that, especially since you're
trying to cut the budget. The others quit so you
didn't owe them anything. Frankly, I'm
surprised you don't remember this since you
guys wrote the contract. That's what the city
attorney says. But, if that's what you want to
do, so be it. Though you might want to
reconsider. I haven't been here long, but I have
been here long enough to gather —

BILL
Our letter demanding your resignation will be
on your desk tomorrow.

CHARLIE
(to Bill)
— a few facts. Like the fact that your brother's
a roofer.

BILL
So what?

CHARLIE
Interesting how he won the bid to repair this
school's roof even though he had the highest
bid, don't you think? That's just the tip of a
really messy iceberg—

RON

Get to the point!

CHARLIE

I've uncovered what could be construed as
payoffs, high-paying contracts, shoddy or non-
existent work, and I've barely scratched the
surface. You boys have been on the School
Board a long time.

WALTER

Are you accusing us—

CHARLIE

I'm not accusing anyone of anything.
    (beat)
Yet.
You want to shut this pageant down? Then go
on stage right now and do it. But remember
this: this pageant makes people happy, it
teaches the kids teamwork and builds up their
self-esteem. Isn't that our goal? You don't get
good citizens from just reading, writing and
arithmetic. It's a new day, gentlemen. I suggest
you go have your board meeting, but instead
of firing me, rethink your goals and your
budgets. I'll cut mine, but no more than the
twelve percent I proposed for this year. I'm
sure if you — if we — work hard enough, we
can all can find a way to reduce expenses.
Unnecessary expense.

BILL

Or you'll do what?

CHARLIE

I don't make threats. Whether you believe it or
not, we're on the same side. Guess you'll have
to chance it. Ready to gamble your political
careers away?

INT. SCHOOL HALL

Charlie leaves the office. Leaves door open. Strides down the hall to auditorium.
Doesn't look back.

INT. SCHOOL AUDITORIUM — BACKSTAGE

The pageant has started, Carole in the wings. Charlie joins her.

> CAROLE
> Where have you been?

> CHARLIE
> Destroying my career.

The pageant progresses. Carole is everywhere.

Charlie stays in one position, watches everything from the wings.

Lindy comes up and stands by her father. Waits for her entrance. Just before she goes
on—

> CHARLIE
> Break a leg.

> LINDY
> (grinning broadly)
> Thanks, Dad.

Lindy goes on stage. Santa follows her on stage. The crowd roars and claps seeing
Santa.

A student comes up to Charlie, looks all around.

> STUDENT
> Have you seen Miss Ringer?

Charlie looks around.

> CHARLIE
> Not in the last few minutes. Can I help?

STUDENT
There's a phone call for her.

CHARLIE
I'll take it.

Charlie moves into the corner of the wing where there's a phone.

CHARLIE
Hello.

EXT. PHONE BOOTH SOMEWHERE — NIGHT

A rotund man with a full white beard is part way in the phone booth.

A yellow light from a AAA truck lights the area. Another man is bent at a car's tire, replacing a flat tire for a good one.

MAN
Tell Carole her Santa got a flat tire. I'll be there
in another couple minutes.

Without waiting for an answer, he hangs up the phone, leaves the phone booth.

INT. SCHOOL AUDITORIUM — BACKSTAGE

The phone at his ear, Charlie spins and looks on stage where Santa performs.

Not taking his gaze off Santa, Charlie hangs up the phone and moves back into the wings.

Carole joins him.

CAROLE
Who was that on the phone? Anything I
should know about?

His eyes still on Santa—

CHARLIE

Yeah, that was your Santa saying he has a flat
tire and he'll be here in a minute.

Puzzled, Carole looks toward the stage and the Santa on stage.

CAROLE

Then who's that?

CHARLIE

You tell me.

INT. SCHOOL AUDITORIUM — FROM AUDIENCE POV

Santa finishes putting his presents under the tree. He steps center stage, waves at the
audience.

SANTA

Ho, ho, ho. Merry Christmas to all and to all a
Good Night!

The crowd roars with approval, clapping.

INT. SCHOOL AUDITORIUM — BACKSTAGE

Santa exits the stage and starts past Charlie and Carole.

CAROLE

Santa!

Santa turns.

Carole starts to say something, stops, then grins.

CAROLE

Merry Christmas, Santa.

SANTA

Merry Christmas, Carole.

Santa pinches her cheek.

SANTA
You too, Charlie. Look for my present under
your tree.

Santa leaves.

CHARLIE
Who was that really?

Carole looks at him and smiles.

Tom, the male lead suddenly comes off the stage, clutching his stomach.

TOM
(in obvious pain)
Miss Ringer, I can't finish. I feel sick.

He covers his mouth.

Charlie signals to another student.

CHARLIE
Help Tom to the bathroom.

Carole grabs the hat and cape off Tom, as he and the other student leave. Carole looks
around anxiously.

CAROLE
We can't stop now. We're almost finished with
Tom's last speech.

CHARLIE
Who else knows the part?

CAROLE
(looks around)
No one.

She looks at him.

CAROLE

Except you.

She puts the hat on his head.

CHARLIE

No way. Those are kids on stage.

She puts the cape around his shoulders.

CAROLE

We're all kids. Just act like one again. You can
do it.

She pushes him toward the stage.

CAROLE

Just believe. Listen to your heart.

Charlie is suddenly on stage, at the extreme edge. Frozen.

Audience is silent. Kids on stage, one by one, elbow each other until all heads turn
toward him.

Oh, the pressure.

He steps further onto stage.

Everyone waits.

He looks to Carole. With her hands, palms up, she pushes at him, as if to tell him to
move forward.

He takes a deep breath. Looks to the audience.

CHARLIE

Long ago, in a land far away, evergreens and
holly were brought into the house in
celebration of the season. Candles brightened
the darkness. And, in another land where
slaves were many, and other thought their

world was lost—

LINDY
—a child was born.

CHARLIE
The rebirth of a nation.
(beat)
Tonight—

His voice catches. He clears his throat.

CHARLIE
—a time of celebration is before us. To a new
year, a new beginning.

ALL PERSONS ON STAGE
Merry Christmas!

AUDIENCE
Merry Christmas!

Audience bursts into applause.

Someone starts to sing SILENT NIGHT. Everyone joins in.

INT. DINER — NIGHT

Charlie, Carole, and the girls go through the after-pageant crowd to a table in the back.
Everyone congratulates them along the way.

Charlie pulls out a chair for Carole. Rainey and Lindy notice, nudging each other.

Waitress hands them menus, places water in front of them.

WAITRESS
Heard you saved the show, Charlie.

RAINEY
Yeah, he was great. Never saw anything like it.
Like he was meant for the part.

CHARLIE

I was just doing what anyone would have
done.

LINDY

Dad, you were awesome.

WAITRESS

Are you folks ready to order?

LINDY

I am. I'll have two eggs, scrambled, a waffle,
and grits.

CHARLIE

Grits? Since when did you start eating grits?

LINDY

(grins widely)

You were the one who said change is good for
the soul. Didn't you mention something about
new beginnings, too? I figure if we're going to
be living in the South, I better get used to
Southern food.

Charlie and Carole exchange a knowing, but worried look.

EXT. PARKING LOT — NIGHT

Leaving the diner Carole and Charlie trail behind the girls.

CAROLE

When are you are you going to tell her?

CHARLIE

Not until after Christmas. The day after. Now
that we're on winter break, it'll be hard to find
another job like this one. I wonder if the
hardware store is hiring.

                    CAROLE
Office supplies would be a better fit.

                    CHARLIE
Come spend the day with us tomorrow. After
you open presents.

                    CAROLE
Okay. The girls will enjoy it.

INT. CAR — NIGHT

As it moves through town.

                    LINDY
Dad! Stop the car!

Puzzled, he pulls over.

Lindy climbs out of the car. Rainey follows.

Carole opens the door calling out.

                    CAROLE
Girls! Wait!

Then she sees where they're headed. She pokes her head into the car.

                    CAROLE
Park it, Charlie.

                    CHARLIE
Where'd they—

He's cut off when Carole shuts the door, following the girls.

Charlie turns off engine and gets out.

Only then does he see the nearly empty Christmas tree lot across the street. The girls are
out of sight. Carole goes into the fenced-in area.

Charlie reaches the lot. Sees the three of them around a tree. Lindy sees him first.

CENTERED

LINDY
Look, Dad. We have to take it home.

Charlie joins them and looks at the tree. Tall, skinny, skimpy, and misshapen.

CHARLIE
Why this one? We already have one.

RAINEY
It's a Charlie Brown tree, Mr. Dickens.

LINDY
Besides this is our new tradition. Finding a
Charlie Brown tree on Christmas Eve.

RAINEY
We'll put decorated pine cones on it.

LINDY
And tiny colored lights.

Charlie reaches for his wallet.

CHARLIE
(to Carole)
Of course, you realize you and Rainey will
have to help decorate. Can you?

CAROLE
Tonight?

RAINEY
Can we pick up Benny first, Mom? He
shouldn't be alone tonight.

CHARLIE
Sure, we can pick up Benny.

EXT. CAR — NIGHT

Tree tied to the roof, the car moves through the night. Few cars on the road.

INT. CAR

Benny between the girls, wears horns again. Girls sing JINGLE BELLS at the top of their lungs. Carole joins in, nudges Charles. He sings too.

INT. LIVING ROOM — NIGHT

Room a mess. String of lights wrapped around BENNY, but he's content chewing on a bone.

Charlie and Carole decorating the tree. Carole looks around.

Carole nudges Charlie and points behind him. Charlie looks.

Both girls on the sofa. Asleep.

> CHARLIE
> Looks like Santa's little elves are plum
> tuckered out.

Carole sets down the decorations in her hands.

> CAROLE
> Guess it's time I take her home.

> CHARLIE
> No need. Let her stay the night. For that matter
> why don't you stay too. We've got a spare
> bedroom.

> CAROLE
> I couldn't do that.

> CHARLIE
> Why not? Don't tell me it isn't proper. Who
> would know?
> (softly)

Besides, I want you to. You can sleep in the
guest room at the top of the stairs.

She and Charlie share a long look.

> CAROLE

All right.

Charlie goes to the sofa and shakes both the girls.

> CHARLIE

Come on, girls. Time for bed.

Lindy and Rainey wake up, yawning. Benny rises too.

> CHARLIE

You and your mother are spending the night
here, Rainey. Come on, let's get you two
upstairs.

The girls get up.

> LINDY

'Night, Dad.

She gives him a kiss. Rainey kisses her mom.

> RAINEY

'Night.

> CHARLIE

Goodnight, girls.

Carole and Charlie go back to decorating the tree.

INT. LINDY'S BEDROOM

Lindy shuts the door. Rainey nearly attacks her, shaking her, jumping up and down.

                    RAINEY
Did you hear that?! Mom is spending the
night!

Tired, Lindy gets her PJs. Then realizes what Rainey just said. She spins around, totally
awed.

                    LINDY
Oh my gosh! It's happening!

Rainey opens a duffle bag. A present is on top.

                    RAINEY
I brought your present.

She pulls her PJs out. Bag is filled with presents.

                    RAINEY
And Mom's too! I brought everything just in
case.

INT. LIVING ROOM

Tree decorated, room cleaned up. Charlie and Carole sit side-by-side on couch. Charlie's
arm draped around Carole, resting on the back of the sofa, his fingers trailing along her
shoulder. Benny at her feet.

                    CHARLIE
So, what did you ask Santa for Christmas?

                    CAROLE
            (surprised)
I thought you didn't believe in Santa.

                    CHARLIE
Not like you. By the way, are you ever going to
tell me who was in the suit tonight?

                    CAROLE
Santa.

CHARLIE

No really.

CAROLE

Really.
(sighs)
One of these days you'll believe.

CHARLIE

Who says I don't. You're here, aren't you?

He starts to lean toward her. Benny jumps up between them, licks them both.

Carole gets up.

CAROLE

Come on, Benny. One last trip out.

Charlie gets up with her.

CHARLIE

I'll take him out for you.

Carole hesitates, then kisses him on the cheek.

CAROLE

Thanks. Night, Charlie.

CHARLIE

Night.

He watches her leave, Benny does too. O.S. her door CLOSES. He shoves his hands into his pockets.

CHARLIE

(to Benny)
Just us guys left now, boy.

Benny's tail thumps. They go through—

INT. KITCHEN

— and out back door.

EXT. YARD

Charlie looks around. Sees nothing. Whistles for Benny.

Just before Charlie closes the back door, he takes one last look.

Nothing.

Slowly, still watching the woods, he shuts the door.

INT. LIVING ROOM

Charlie goes to the tree ready to pull the plug.

He stops and leaves the lights on. Goes to a closet and takes down a stack of packages and arranges them under the tree.

One has Rainey's name on it. Then he takes a small box out of his pocket. For Carole. Puts it under the tree as well.

Turns out the living room light. Tree lights glow softly in the dark.

O.S. Charlie's STEPS on staircase.

Benny hears something outside. Goes to the window and looks out. Nothing there.

INT. UPSTAIRS HALLWAY

Charlie hesitates, hand still on the stair handrail. He sees the light under Carole's door go out.

He continues on to his room.

INT. LINDY'S BEDROOM

LINDY
Ssshhhh. I hear him coming.

Rainy and Lindy listen as Charlie's FOOTSTEPS pass her door.

O.S. Door CLOSES.

They wait a few more seconds, then both scramble out of bed. Using flashlights, Lindy goes to her closet and gets a small pile of presents.

Rainey retrieves her bag from beside the bed and opens it.

                    RAINEY
          What'd you get your dad?

                    LINDY
          A sweater. What'd you get your mom?

                    RAINEY
     A T-shirt.

Packages in hands, they sneak downstairs. Place packages under tree. Scurry back upstairs.

INT. UPSTAIRS HALLWAY

No sooner does their door closes, then Carole's door opens. Her arms ladened with gifts. She goes downstairs—

INT. LIVING ROOM

— and puts them under the tree.

Benny thumps tail seeing her. She pats him on head.

                    CAROLE
          Good boy. Guard the tree.

Benny thumps his tail again.

O.S. Steps on staircase. Door CLOSES.

Benny settles his head between paws again. House is quiet. CLOCK TICKS.

O.S. MOTOR OF CAR, driving past.

Quiet again.

Benny's head jerks up.

BENNY'S POV from floor level: Door knob moves. Benny cocks his head one way, then another.

Door opens. Benny sits up.

Black boots, red pants, walk into the house. Gloved hand pats Benny on head.

Benny watches as several gifts— unwrapped but with tags— are placed under the tree.

A Christmas water globe for Lindy.

A music box for Rainey.

A tote bag with a huge apple core for Carole.

And a red, Christmas themed canister for Charlie.

Gloved hand tapes an envelope to the wheeled sled that is placed behind the tree, nearly out of sight, propping it again the wall. Addressed to Charlie. Return address is Alaska. Envelope beaten and worn, lots of post office red-ink stamped on it. Old stamp.

Gloved hand pats Benny on head again. Boots leave the room.

Door CLICKS SOFTLY closed.

Benny goes to window and looks out. Tail wags.

INT. KITCHEN — EARLY MORNING

Charlie enters kitchen. Finds Carole already there. At the table drinking coffee.

> CHARLIE
> Couldn't sleep either?

> CAROLE
> Habit. Rainey's usually the first one up on
> Christmas, though.

> CHARLIE
> They were up late. I heard them sneaking
> downstairs.

Carole smiles.

> CAROLE
> So did I. Coffee's made.

> CHARLIE
> Thanks.

He gets a cup and joins her at the table.

> CHARLIE
> You always look this good in the morning?

Carole laughs.

> CAROLE
> You really didn't get much sleep, did you?

> CHARLIE
> Actually—

Both girls blast into the kitchen, instantly tugging on their parents.

> LINDY
> It's time to open presents!

> RAINEY
> Hurry up, you two!

INT. LIVING ROOM

Carole and Charlie sit on sofa. Girls start handing them presents.

Carole opens the package from Charlie. It's a ladybug pin and she promptly puts it on.

> CAROLE
> I love it. Thank you.

                    CHARLIE
          You're welcome. Bugs.

Girls exchange knowing looks and smile.

INT. LIVING ROOM — MINUTES LATER

Paper everywhere. Each holds Santa's gift, though Charlie hasn't opened the canister
yet.

                    CAROLE
          Come on, Charlie. Confess. You got me this
          tote. Not the traditional teacher's apple, is it?

                    CHARLIE
          I swear I didn't.

                    CAROLE
          Rainey?

                    RAINEY
          Really, Mom. I didn't either.

                    LINDY
          Don't look at me.

Lindy sees the sled behind the tree. Brings it out.

Everyone stops and stares.

                    LINDY
              (fingering envelope)
          Look, Dad. This is for you.

Charlie gets up, removes envelope from the sled. Stares at it like he's seen a ghost.

                    CHARLIE
          It's my father's handwriting. Dated the year
          after he left.

He opens it. Silently, he starts to read, then stops. He can't. He hands it to Carole.

> **CAROLE**
> Dear Charlie. I don't know how to tell you this,
> so I'll just come out and say it. I was wrong. I
> was hurting that day I told you not to believe
> in Christmas. It was the most miserable day of
> my life when I left you and your mother. None
> of it was your fault. I want you to know that.
> And that reindeer you saw — it was real. I saw
> it too, when I was a boy.

Lindy and Rainey exchange looks. Carole stares at Charlie. Then, continues to read —

> **CAROLE**
> Without magic, there is no sparkle in our lives.
> Forgive me, son. Love Dad.

Carole hands the letter back to Charlie. Charlie lays it on the table and gets up, goes to the window.

Rainey and Lindy look at each other, then toward Carole.

The DOORBELL RINGS.

Charlie looks toward it and frowns.

> **CHARLIE**
> Who in the world?

He looks to Carole. She shakes her head, lifts her shoulders.

INT. FRONT DOOR

He opens the door. It's Ron.

> **CHARLIE**
> (with flat voice)
> Merry Christmas, Ron.

                    RON
Can I talk to you for a minute? I'm sorry to
interrupt your holiday. Out here?

EXT. PORCH

Ron backs up. Charlie follows.

                    RON
My wife threatened to leave if I didn't make
the right decision. I'll be talking to the Board
next week. We need you here more than we
knew.
          (he smiles and offers his hand)
Merry Christmas, Charlie.

Charlie shakes his hand, watches Ron leave.

It starts to snow. He looks up at the sky in wonder, grinning.

INT. LIVING ROOM

He's barely back inside, when Lindy propels herself into him, hugging him tightly.

                    LINDY
We're staying?

                    CHARLIE
We're staying. And I've got a special Christmas
present for you.
          (beat)
It's snowing outside.

All three girls exclaim at once, crowd around the window.

Lindy and Rainey race for the back door. Carole takes Charlie's hand.

                    CAROLE
Come on. We can't miss this!

EXT. BACK YARD

Snow so thick it's nearly impossible to see across the yard.

The girls dance in it. Carole sticks out her tongue catching flakes. Charlie holds out his hand, catches flakes, looks up at the sky.

> CHARLIE
> This is ridiculous. It's too warm to snow.

> CAROLE
> For once in your life Charlie, do something
> smart.

> CHARLIE
> What's that?

> CAROLE
> Don't question it. Just accept it. Accept this,
> too.

Carole grabs him, wraps her arms around his neck, pulls him down and kisses him. Charlie wraps his arms around her, lifts her off her feet.

Lindy and Rainey grin from ear to ear. They go back inside leaving the two adults alone.

Finally, the kiss ends. Their foreheads rest against each other.

> CAROLE
> Merry Christmas, Charlie.

> CHARLIE
> Merry Christmas. Tell me something. Who was
> your number one choice?

> CAROLE
> Don't you know by now? It was always you.

CHARLIE
(grinning)
Does this mean we're dating and exclusive?

CAROLE
What do you think?

They walk inside arm in arm.

INT. LIVING ROOM

Rainey shuts her music box seeing Carole and Charlie. Lindy stops shaking her globe. Sets it down.

Lindy spots the unopened canister and grabs it.

LINDY
Dad, you never opened your last gift!

He grabs his clipboard.

CHARLIE
Today—

Carole grabs the clipboard and tosses it behind her back, not caring where it lands.

CHARLIE
Hey! You can't take that away.

CAROLE
You're going to be too busy to notice you're not organized anymore.

Carole kisses Charlie again.

Girls hi-five each other. Benny jumps around, barking.

In the process, the canister falls and crashes to the floor, spilling open. Magic dust. Lindy and Rainy see it. Scoop it up and fling it into the air.

LINDY
Look it's snowing inside!

They laugh. The girls hug their parents.

EXT. YARD

From the edge of the woods, Bently's POV through the window. Christmas tree lights and the sparkle fairy dust as it flies through the air.

It starts snowing again.

Bently's last look before disappearing into the woods: A family enjoying the magic of Christmas.

FADE OUT

ABOUT THE AUTHOR

Diana Stout, MFA, Ph.D. is an award-winning screenwriter, author, who became a published author before returning to school and becoming an English professor, where she taught various writing classes. Her students would say, "She smiles when she talks about writing." Published in multiple genres, Dr. Stout has written fiction—long and short, published magazine articles and short stories, is a former magazine and newspaper columnist, optioned a Hollywood screenplay, and had several short plays produced in New York city. She's served as a writing contest judge for various organizations, as an editor, and enjoys helping other writers learn the craft. Today, she writes full-time and is an indie publisher through her company, Sharpened Pencils Productions LLC. When not writing, she enjoys watching movies, reading, and jigsaw puzzles.

OTHER TITLES

Grendel's Mother

Shattered Dreams: A Laurel Ridge Novella (#1)

Burning Desire: A Laurel Ridge Novella (#2)

Arrested Pleasures: A Laurel Ridge Novella (#3)

Buried Hearts: A Laurel Ridge Novella (#4)

Tangled Passions: A Laurel Ridge Novella (#5)

Determined Hearts

Love's New Beginnings

Tomorrow's Wish for Love

Maggie's Story

The Super Simple Easy Basic Cookbook

David & Goliath – a screenplay

Lost and Found – an anthology (contributor & editor)

FOLLOW DIANA STOUT

Website: sharpenedpencilsproductions.com
Facebook: facebook.com/DianaStoutScreenwriterAuthor
Twitter: twitter.com/ScreenWryter13
Pinterest: pinterest.com/drdianastout
Goodreads goodreads.com/user/show/43124185-diana-stout
Instagram: instagram.com/authordianastout
BookBub: bookbub.com/authors/diana-stout

Blogs

Behind the Scenes – life as a writer: dianastout.net
Into the Core – paranormal experiences: dianastout.com
Featured Guests with Diana Stout: dianastout.org

Join My Facebook Group

I invite you to join my private Facebook group: Diana's Dynamos
– fans, followers, readers & writers.

The group is private where only members can see who's in the
group and what they post.

Your joining is an indication that you'll support my publications
by word-of-mouth, share my posts, and provide reviews when
reading my books.

I encourage your questions and welcome your participation.

To join, click or use this URL.
https://www.facebook.com/groups/1154207845314046

Can You Help Me, Please?

Can you leave me a quick review online where you obtain your books?

Writing a review helps me find more readers.

Providing a review is the best way for a reader to thank the author.

Reviews can be short!
- I loved this book!
- I like this book!
- I couldn't put this book down!

It's not the length of a review that counts; it's the number of reviews a book receives that's important.

THANK YOU!